Twilight Moon

David Stocks

chipmunkapublishing
the mental health publisher

Published by
Chipmunkapublishing
United Kingdom

http://www.chipmunkapublishing.com

ISBN   978-1-78382-000-9

Chipmunkapublishing gratefully acknowledge the support of Arts Council England.

David Stocks

To Jules, My Guardian Angel

Chapter 1 – A Walk in the Woods

The trees seemed different as twilight embraced the woods, their autumnal colours tinged by a cool electric blue. A full moon shone blue, adding to the eerie light. Indeed the leaves crackled underfoot like an electric current, as Trinity and I made our way deeper into the woodland.

Trinity is a brindle coloured three-legged Staffordshire bull terrier, a rescue dog, with a chequered past. I found her at the vets, still with her stitches in from an operation to remove her cancerous leg. She hopped her way around the counter and gave me her best doe-eyed look; her huge sad eyes captured my heart. The last time I had seen that look I ended up getting engaged; this time the vet casually mentioned she needed a home and that was that. I could no longer leave her homeless than hand back a million pound lottery win. It was a decision that I have never regretted; a decision that has profoundly changed my life for the better.

They say that dogs resemble their owners and I guess that could be true in a way of Trinity and me. I have a stocky build like a Staffie and flecked brown hair that resembles her coat. My eyes are hazel though, where Trinity's are deep brown pools of canine intelligence. Yet still, as we walked through the woods, we looked as one; man and dog. But who was the master?

A low mist hovered over the forest floor, just high enough to hide my feet as it swirled around Trinity and me, tinged with a twilight blue haze. Suddenly a huge red stag appeared in front of us, its giant hooves skipping silently across the mist seemingly not touching the ground. I had never seen deer here before and nor had Trinity, who was off after it like a shot as it disappeared into the trees beyond. In vain I called after my vanishing faithful companion: "Stay!" - Although I already knew my command would have no effect as I strained to keep pace with her. It never ceased to amaze me how fast she could run for a three-legged dog!

Deeper and deeper into the woods we ran, all the time the woodland getting denser, making it hard to weave a path in and out of the trees. I have regularly walked through these woods and thought I had explored every inch of them; I couldn't remember them stretching so far, or so thickly.

Yet still the woodland engulfed us in its leafy grasp with seemingly no end to the trees. The deer had long since gone, but still my three-legged friend charged on. Time seemed to lose all meaning as we ran; for although we had pursued the deer for sometime now, the light hadn't changed and twilight had taken an eternal hold over the woods.

As Trinity bounded ahead of me she appeared like a dolphin, her head disappearing under the blue mist only to reappear seconds later as she emerged. In fact it felt as if I was swimming through the trees with a current pushing along behind us. Although we had been running now for quite some time my legs didn't get tired and my feet barely felt as if they touched the ground.

I knew now that we were lost, but Trinity had just one thing on her mind: a certain red stag which had long since disappeared from sight. This did not perturb Trinity though; her canine hunting powers were surely a match for a giant red stag! Her acute sense of smell must still have scent of the stag; her acute hearing seemed to have failed her, however, as she continually ignored my cries for her to stop.

Stop she did eventually when we came to a fast flowing river; even her canine superpowers were not strong enough for her to cross this raging torrent. River, what river? I had never seen or heard of a river in this area. Looking downstream the river tumbled over a roaring waterfall; surely I would have heard of a mighty waterfall in the region? I was lost and puzzled as we stood there panting on the banks of this mysterious river. Where was I? How did we get here? More to the question: how do we get back?

I looked around but I couldn't see the path on which we had arrived. Across the river I could see smoke curling into the twilight sky which was surely a sign of habitation. "But how do we get there?" I asked myself.

There was only one thing for it: We couldn't go downstream as that led to a crushing waterfall and steep cliffs; we would have to walk along the banks upstream until we found a way to cross. If there was such a thing?

Now that we were lost in a forgotten part of the forest the swirling mist that covered the forest floor had dispersed, almost as if it had done its job in getting us here. As we walked along the banks of the river under a canopy of overhanging trees, twilight still held its grip on the day; even though it felt as if it had been a number of hours since we first set out on this treacherous trail.

What strangeness was in the air that held us in this twilight embrace? I am no believer in magic, yet I could see no logic as to how time itself was held in limbo and the laws of physics ceased to exist in this timeless place. Could there be magic in the air? What superstitious nonsense was I now thinking? I looked at Trinity and she rolled her huge eyes. I knew what that meant: 'Okay master I know I led us here; now you get us back.' Oh, to have such a trusting and loyal companion!

My thoughts turned to my wife who must by now be fretting at home. I tried to phone her on my mobile phone, but as so often in the countryside there was no signal. Mobile phones are mobile so long as you are close to major areas of habitation. This I most certainly was not. I was pleased to have Trinity with me; otherwise my loneliness in this begotten place may well have got the better of me. I have a bipolar mental health condition, which means my mood can swing dramatically up or down. At the moment it was teetering on the downwards side. Trinity with her canine instinct knew this and stayed close by my side. I am her protector, but she is also mine.

I reigned in my wandering thoughts for we had a situation to get ourselves out of, which was mainly to cross this river and seek help. I considered swinging Tarzan-like from a branch across the river, but thankfully my rational side stopped me pursuing this further; that and the minor issue of transporting a three-legged dog via this method.

As it happened there was no need to adopt such a dramatic system of crossing the river, for as we rounded a bend in the river I spied stepping stones put there for the purpose. The stepping stones turned out to be rough hewn boulders, many of which were partly submerged in the water. I have crossed rivers using stepping stones before, but not when they are partly submerged with a strong current raging around them. I looked at Trinity who gazed back trustingly with her big brown eyes. I knew what that meant; yes she would cross the river if her master would be kind enough to transport her in his arms. I beckoned for her to cross, to which she rolled her eyes in bewilderment. There was only one thing for it, but I wasn't over confident in my ability to get us both across.

I gently lifted Trinity wriggling and kicking into my arms, where she then settled trustingly, all three stones of her. With little or no choice as to the fate that lay ahead of me, I stepped on to the first stone as water raged around my boots. So far, so good. I strode forward onto the next stone, which tilted at an alarming angle, forcing me to quickly step onto the following stone to stop me, dog and all falling into the river. I watched as the bolder tumbled and sank behind me. Great, no way back now! I felt as if some invisible presence was forcing us further and further on this journey. Trying not to think about the close shave I had just had, I continued on my way across the slippery stones. What a sight we must have made; a man teetering across stepping stones carrying a substantial dog. Throwing caution to the wind I quickened my gait, wanting to get this troublesome crossing over with. Faster and faster I went, with Trinity burying her head in my arms, not daring to look. I slipped more than once but somehow I made it over to the other side, more by luck than judgement.

I gently put Trinity down upon the shore, relieved that somehow I had got us both safely across. Now all we had to do was head towards the smoke trails in the sky. Once I had found habitation, a quick phone call and we could be picked up by my wife and taken home. That was the plan at least.

I chose a trail that went into the forest in roughly the right direction for the smoke, this time with Trinity following close behind me and not vice versa. It was good to see that she respected her master now that she had got us lost.

Autumn leaves piled high on the path before us, their oranges and golds cast with a bluish tinge from the twilight sky. As we kicked our way through them they rippled like blue-tipped flames from the forest floor. Everything around us was surreal; somehow not real in the sense of the modern world, but something more ancient and beyond our imagination. Trees twisted their sinewy forms in cloaks of red and gold, dancing in the wind to the rustling sound of autumn. Where had this wind come from? Before we crossed the river there had been no wind. Now it swirled in eddies around us, spinning leaves around in kaleidoscopic displays of colour and light. Faster and stronger the wind blew around us, swirling the leaves in an autumnal fiesta, crackling like fire and brushing our bodies with their crisp autumn fingers.

I soon lost all sense of direction, no longer sure which way the smoke lay. Trinity stayed close to me, fearful of the maelstrom of leaves. Still I kept walking as if being pushed by the leaves, joining them in their autumn dance. I had no idea of where we were going, but by taking the path of least resistance I hoped we would eventually reach some kind of civilisation. Without hope there is no light; only darkness and the descent into depression that so often grips me. Hope is my guiding lantern in the darkness, or in this case, a path through autumn's veil to safety beyond.

'What lay beyond?' was a question of which I was not certain; or indeed was an answer that I wanted to know. There was something unnatural about these woods and the never-ending twilight that embraced them. Good or bad, I was not sure which, but I could sense both in the air; I just hoped that when we emerged from this carnival of leaves it would be to something good and not bad. For the bad was like a darkness stalking us, waiting for its turn to strike at our fearful hearts and engulf us in misery and despair.

Trinity sensed it too, fear clearly showing in the whites of her eyes, her body pressing against my legs. Fear not what you can see but what you can't see. These were the words that ran through my head as we made our way further through the trees and the leaves. As if I had summoned it I heard a distant howl upon the wind, sending shivers down my spine and causing Trinity to bark at our unseen foe.

While the howl was still echoing in my ears the wind began to die down, the leaves tumbling once more to the forest floor. The howl seemed to command the elements and caused the wind to stop. Now there was only silence, louder than any noise. I could hear my heart beat inside my eardrums and stood rooted to the spot, fearful to go on.

It was then that I heard laughter coming from above; a deep belly laughter, mocking and taunting. Nervously I looked up to behold the source of the laughter. I wished I hadn't, for perched on a branch above me was what I can only describe as a leprechaun. Well if he wasn't a leprechaun he was certainly making a good impression of one, from the curled up boots, green britches, silver buckle and red waistcoat, to a pointed green hat with a bell on. He had a fat belly and a long white beard. Was my mind playing games with me? Was this a symptom of my bipolar? I was not sure.

Slowly, but surely, my elfin friend stopped laughing and then with a twinkle in his eye said, "Welcome to Twilight Wood my friends. You must have crossed over from the world of man. Long may your stay be here and may the twilight beast spare you."

Chapter 2 – The Mysterious Glade

I looked at the leprechaun who was no taller than a child and replied, "I was hoping my stay was going to be short; can you tell us the way back please?"
"Ah, that's not so easy now is it, with the moon and twilight being what it is."

I looked at the moon, which hung blue in the twilight sky and questioned, "What's the moon and twilight got to do with it?"

"The twilight moon is the time to cross; return too soon and you will be lost."

I had by now had enough of this cryptic Leprechaun and retorted, "Can you tell us the way back or not?"

"What's the rush? Enjoy your stay but just watch out for the beast I pray."

Then with a flash our cheeky little friend on the branch was gone.

My rational mind told me I must be seeing things; psychotic illusions can be one of the symptoms of bipolar. Yet I had never experienced such vivid and real illusions in the past. Still I questioned my sanity, refusing to believe what I had seen and heard was real. I looked down at Trinity for reassurance, only to find she was gazing back up at me with her faithful eyes, seemingly unperturbed by our recent encounter. It was great to have such a trusting dog; the only problem was that right now I didn't trust my mind and could no longer distinguish between what was real and unreal.

"Right," I said more to myself than Trinity, "let's find our way out of here."

We were now in a glade with a grassy hummock in its centre. Just a short climb and we should have a good view over the forest.

I beckoned Trinity to follow and started climbing the mound. All at once I heard the sounds of small bells tinkling around us. Psychosis seemed to be taking hold of my mind, with unreal sounds and visions plaguing me. I looked at Trinity who seemed oblivious to the bells and kept climbing. The further we climbed, the more bells I heard. I became more and more convinced that I was losing my mind especially when I heard the sounds of laughter, sweet and clear around me.

What madness is this that I hear bells and laughter, yet see nothing but grass and trees?

A flash of light caught my eye but was gone before I could focus on it. I turned hoping to see where it had gone, but nothing was there. Soon I began glimpsing more flashes of light but was never able to see what was causing it. The light seemed to be accompanied by more sweet laughter, almost as if it was mocking me. I tried to ignore it and kept walking up the hillock. How far had I travelled from the real world since setting off on this twilight walk?

As I neared the top of the hillock daisies and buttercups appeared amongst the grass, which were most unusual for this time of year. What awaited me at the top was even more extraordinary though. As I rounded the top of the hillock before me was what I could only describe as a fairy court. Sat upon a buttercup throne was the fairy queen in gowns of gossamer and gold. All around her was the fairy court, resplendent in yellow tunics and silver dresses. The fairies flew around the hill top with translucent wings shimmering like rainbows in the moonlight. Tiny bells tinkled attached to hats and dresses and there was laughter all around. Each fairy was only a few inches high; no bigger than a large butterfly.

"Welcome to my fairy mound mortals. What brings you to twilight woods this eve?" greeted the queen in a chiming voice.

"Err ... Hello your majesty," I answered hesitantly. "We got lost in the woods and do not know how we came here."

"You were found then my mortal friends. Was it a deer perchance?"

"A red stag, tall and proud!" I exclaimed. "Trinity chased it and now we are here."
"The stag is a creature of two worlds and can cross over on a twilight moon. The stag found you and brought you here; for what purpose I currently don't know."

"How, may I ask, are we to get back?"

"Return you shall, but not yet I am afraid. There is a reason for you being here and until your purpose has been resolved, here you shall stay."

"Cannot the red stag lead us back?"

"He is lord of two worlds and will only return when he feels you have achieved that which is set out for you."

"You speak in riddles," I sighed.

"You have much to learn dear friend and riddles are the magic of these woods. Follow the turtle - we have to fly - the turtle will take you onwards on your journey; goodbye."

The queen then turned her head to the sky and flapped her wings in the silvery light. With an escort of fairies she flew up high and disappeared into a trail of starry light.

I looked at Trinity, at a loss from this latest encounter. Trinity rolled her big brown eyes as if in agreement.

I refused to believe this latest encounter and greatly feared my senses were betraying me. Perhaps madness had descended and I had lost touch with reality. What was real and not real I was now not certain. Of riddles and turtles I was even less sure. How were we to follow a turtle?

"Humph", a deep voice echoed through the ground. "Freeloaders, get off my back!"

"What ... who's that?" I struggled to answer.

"Exactly the same question I was about to ask you."

"Err ... Just one man and his dog, lost in the woods."

"Lost eh, well then perhaps I can help."

All of a sudden the ground moved beneath us, sending us sprawling on the grassy hillock. The hill was rising up from the ground. Then from the bottom of the hill out shot a wizened head. The head then turned and looked up at us.

"In answer to your question, I am a turtle and I'd rather you didn't climb upon my shell."

"A shell? I thought you were a hill with grass and flowers upon it?"

"A hill! How demeaning!" grunted the turtle indignantly. "I am tempted to throw you off and crush you into the ground!"

"S ... sorry, noble turtle. I ... I didn't mean to offend. It is just I have never come across a turtle so large before."

"Noble, now I like that. Perhaps you are not so bad after all."

"Can you help us, kind turtle sir? We are lost and need to find our way home."

"Lost eh, you're mortals aren't you?"

"Err, yes, in the fact that we live and die. Although I would rather not die just yet."

"Well then, perhaps I can help. I can take you onwards, but I can't take you home though."

"But we need to get home," I reasoned.

"That's as maybe, but you need to go forwards to go back."

"Oh, more riddles, when will they end?"

"It's your choice: You can journey with me, or you can get off my shell and find your own way."

I looked down at Trinity who looked back up at me faithfully.

"Well, if you put it like that, could we ride a while upon your beautiful shell?"

"Why of course, hold on tight, here we go."

Twilight Moon

Chapter 3 – The Fire Swamp

With a "Humph" the turtle eased itself forward with its cargo of bewildered travellers into the trees beyond.

"Where are we going?" I asked somewhat tentatively.

"To the Oracle of course! Only the Oracle can tell you the reason why you are here."

"Where does the Oracle live?" I questioned.

"On the Lake of a Thousand Souls," replied the turtle in a deep booming dramatic voice.

"Oh," I sighed, I wished I'd never asked!

As the turtle moved through autumn's rusty carpet of leaves I was amazed to see fresh grass shoot up wherever the turtle stepped and spring flowers sprout all around. The turtle was laying its own path of spring. From the tinkle of bells and the sweet sound of laughter all around I realised this had to be fairy magic, but also that the turtle must be a very blessed creature indeed. I revelled in the beauty of it all, but in the back of my mind was fear of our destination: The Lake of a Thousand Souls. What could it be?

I still struggled with reason; this surely couldn't be happening. How could Trinity and I be riding a giant turtle who turned all it touched into spring? This was not rational; surely my mind was playing tricks on me? It was difficult to ignore the evidence of my eyes though no matter how hard I tried to deny it.

Curious and fearful at the same time, I asked the turtle, "Is it far to the Lake of a Thousand Souls?"

The reply wasn't exactly what I was hoping for.

"Yes, it is a long journey and to reach it we must first pass through the treacherous fire swamps."

"Err, is it absolutely necessary to visit the Oracle?" I asked, already knowing what answer I was likely to get.

"Yes, the Oracle is all seeing and all knowing; you must see the Oracle in order to find out why you are here. If you don't find out why you are here, you will never be able to return home."

Then the turtle added, as if by consolation, "It's not far to the fire swamps though."

"Oh great," I muttered.

Trinity rolled her big brown eyes at me; I'm sure she understands every word I say.

Soon the woods began to thin out and the ground became boggier; even the turtle's magic fail to turn this mud into grass and flowers, but still the turtle trudged on. A foul smell soon permeated the air; from where it came I was not sure.
"What is that awful smell?" I asked the turtle.

"Oh, that's just the fire swamps ahead of us, all sulphur and brimstone you know."

"Great," I muttered again.

"Have you ever crossed the fire swamps before?" I enquired.

"Oh no, never dared; not many creatures who venture in survive the fire swamp."

"Brilliant! Is there another way perhaps?"

"No, sadly not," came the ominous reply. "You will have to be our lookout as you have the best vantage point from up there," he continued.

"Err, what do I look out for exactly?"

"Smoke of course! Don't you know there is no smoke without fire? If you see smoke then fire is sure to follow. Try and guide me where there is no smoke and then we won't have a swamp full of turtle soup, hey."

"Or hot dog or chargrilled human," I replied.

It wasn't long before the stench became overpowering and the boggy mud turned to swamp. A mist rose from the swamp, yellow vapours turning green in the blue twilight light. Rotting trees protruded from the swamp like skeletal fingers clawing at the sky. The swamp stretched as far as the eye could see with pillars of fire shooting up randomly from its sickly surface. Now, I thought, would be a good time to turn back.

"No going back now," said the turtle as it pushed its way into the ooze.

"Great." I muttered, yet again.

"Hold on tight, we have to go fast or get roasted."

The turtle surged ahead through the slime and sludge with an amazing turn of speed.

"Smoke ahead", I yelled, as a plume of smoke erupted just ahead.

Nimbly, for a turtle of his size, the turtle swerved to the right, just in time as a flame blasted upwards to our left.

"Woof," barked Trinity, just as another smoke stream appeared ahead. That dog must have a sixth sense or something, I thought and yelled, "Smoke ahead," again.
"If Trinity bark's turn left or right," I think she knows when the smoke is coming."

"Will do," answered the turtle, "dogs have amazing senses."

As if to emphasize the fact Trinity barked again and the Turtle swerved just in time, the hairs on my arms feeling singed from the heat. What followed was a series of "Woof," "Smoke" commands in that order, followed by a surge to the left or right, as pillars of flame tried to engulf us. I expected Robin to pop up and say "Holy smoke!" at anytime.

All was going well until a whole line of smoke appeared before us. Quickly I shouted, "Stop!"

The turtle applied reverse flippers as quick as he could and we only just stopped in time, but how were we going to pass all these flame vents?

When the flames sank back down again I counted how long before the next flames appeared. Just six seconds. Could we make it through in that time?

"When the flames die down", I said to the turtle, "go forward as quickly as you can; we only have six seconds. Can you make it?"

"I think I can. Here we go!"

"Whoa, Woof," we shouted and barked in unison as the turtle surged forward with such speed that we both ended up on our backs. Still we only just made it in time and I noticed the grass at the back of the turtle's shell got singed.

"Wow, that was a close call," I had just time to say, before Trinity barked her warning again and the turtle surged to the left.

What followed was a series of frantic barks and turns as we wove an intricate path through the swamp. After a while though the smoke became less and less and we were able to steer a steadier course through the swamp. Eventually the smoke and fire stopped altogether, the swamp drying up and turning to mud once more.

"We made it!" I cried.

"Humph," exclaimed an exhausted turtle as it settled on the mud. "Now all we have to do is cross the Lake of a Thousand Souls, after we have rested of course."

Chapter 4 – The Lake of a Thousand Souls

After a rest we set out again for the lake. The trees began to thicken once more covered in their autumn glory. The path the turtle took started sprouting grass and flowers again. Twilight light suffused the forest lending a blue sheen to the autumn colour.

"What is the Lake of a Thousand Souls?" I tentatively asked.

"It's a deep dark lake," came the reply, "darker than the darkest night, deeper than the highest mountain is high. But that's not all there is to the lake, it is a lake where all the lost souls gather, drowning in eternal woe."
"I know a thing or two about woe," I said, thinking of the lows that have come upon me as a result of my bipolar mental illness.

"That's as maybe, but these souls try to suck the spirit out of you and drag you down with them. Many a voyager has drowned on that lake as a result."

"Are you really sure we have to go there?" I asked pleadingly.

"Oh yes, you must see the Oracle and the Oracle lives on the Lake of a Thousand Souls."

"Cheerful place to live," I muttered.

The journey between the fire swamp and the lake passed without incident. A small respite I knew. Soon however the lake was upon us; I knew we must be approaching the lake as the trees were stripped bare and the flowered path of the turtle disappeared once more.

The lake when we arrived was worse than even my imagination could conjure. The water, if you can call it that, was like a huge black oil slick; blacker than night, blacker than coal; in fact it was so black it was more like an absence of colour where light of any kind failed to escape its dark clutches.

"Keep your eyes shut and your ears covered," advised the turtle. "We are going to cross the lake to the Oracle's island and anything you see or hear could drag you down to its bottomless depths."

With that the turtle launched into the blackness of the lake and we began our voyage to the Oracle's island. Quickly I shut my eyes and covered my ears paying heed to the turtle's advice. Trinity pushed her head beneath my arm, her own senses telling her to take cover now.

Despite having my ears covered I could hear whispering voices emanating from the lake. I tried to ignore them, but they kept coming through.

"Sssss ... Your soul is bad, we are hungry for your soul." Voices hissed all around me.

Visions of everything I had ever done wrong plagued me. My own self worth plummeted. I could feel myself slipping into the inky embrace of the lake.

What right did such a pitiful being such as me have to be alive? I could feel the negative side of my bipolar overtaking me. Why not end it all now and join these lost souls in the lake? Slowly I opened my eyes.

Green eyes stared up at me from the depths of the lake. "Come, come ..." they whispered, "Come and join us, come and join us."

The eyes were mesmerising; they held me in a trance. I could feel myself compelled to dive in and join them. Slowly I stood up and readied myself to leap in. Now was the time to rid the world of my pitiful soul.

Just as I was about to leap I heard a bark; an echo of the past; a long forgotten friend. Who was that friend? My head was all fuzzy.

"Come to us ... come join us in our sorrow," beckoned the voices, stronger now. The green eyes were like tractor beams dragging me down.

Trinity barked again and again, frantic to wake her master. Don't disturb me I thought, not now, when oblivion is so near. But still Trinity barked, until I eventually woke from my trance and stopped just as I was about to leap off the turtle's shell into the dark waters below.

"Trinity," I called and hugged my faithful hound. Her connection to me was stronger than any evil emanating from the lake. "Thank you," I said, "thank you," I repeated several times.

The Lake of a Thousand Souls had nearly claimed me as its latest victim, but it hadn't counted on the strong connection between man and dog. The forsaken souls had lost their grip on me and I was now able to gaze safely across the lake. On the horizon I could now make out an island with white sandy shores and a central mountain. It wasn't long, with the turtle's powerful strokes, before we neared the island. It was like a tropical paradise with palm trees leaning lazily over its beaches and covering the interior mountain. Even the waters cleared into a crystal blue suffused by the light from the blue twilight glow.

"Wow, it's beautiful!" I exclaimed, "Does the island have a name?"

"It is called many things," replied the turtle: "Seeker's Island, Angel's Rest, Summer Island, to name but a few."

"It's hard to believe that such a jewel of an island exists in the middle of such a dark lake," I commented.

"Without darkness there is no light," replied the turtle cryptically.

With those words the turtle made its final approach and drew up on the shore.

"I will rest here while you go and visit the Oracle. You will find his cave at the top of the mountain. Go safely my friends; I will await your return."

"Thank you dear turtle, you have braved much to get us here and are a true friend."

We climbed down off the turtle's back through the spring flowers and walked through the fine white sand towards the island's interior.

At the edge of the beach a path opened up through the thick tropical vegetation. We followed the path as it climbed towards the mountain; multicoloured flowers hung over our heads as we made our way up with humming birds sipping their sweet nectar. In the distance we could hear the sound of monkeys calling. We passed pools full of giant lily pads with frogs croaking their evening song. This was indeed a tropical paradise.

The walk to the mountain passed without incident, but when we arrived at the mountainside proper we realised the enormity of the task that lay ahead of us. The mountainside was sheer, way too steep to climb, with no obvious path up. How were we to get up?

We circled the perimeter of the mountain but all the slopes remained the same, steep and inaccessible. Frustrated we stopped by a pool for a drink, Trinity lapping up the water happily. In the middle of the pool there were giant spherical flowers, like huge paper balloons on long green stalks. Trinity by this time had become too hot and dived in the pool for a swim. Feeling the heat myself I followed her in.

Trinity scrambled up onto one of the giant lily pads in the middle of the pond and I followed her on. We sat their together on our lily pad boat with a giant orange flower floating above us. Trinity, who loves playing with sticks, took the giant stalk of the flower for a stick and grabbed it in her powerful jaws. With a crunch the stalk broke in two with Trinity hanging on to the top half of it. What happened next totally surprised me. The flower acted like a giant helium balloon and started lifting Trinity off the lily pad. Quickly I grabbed hold of it to try and bring her back down. This didn't quite have the desired effect as we were both lifted into the air.

Higher and higher we went, spiralling in a hot air current, the tropical forest disappearing behind us. The air current took us up over the mountain top. I realised I had to do something quickly. I remembered my trusty penknife that I always carried with me and took it out of my pocket with my free hand, flicked open the blade and quickly slashed the balloon flower. The flower popped and with a bang dropped us on the mountain top but only just in time, as any further and we would have fallen to our deaths. We had arrived in a slightly unexpected style at the top of the mountain and before us was a cave. This must be where the Oracle lives.

Chapter 5 – The Oracle

Having brushed ourselves down after our unexpected flight we walked over to the cave. From inside there came a warming glow. Seeing as there was no door on which to knock we moved inside the entrance and I called, "Hello, anybody there?" My voice echoed around the cave.
"Hello," I repeated, which itself repeated in echoes.

"What, who's there?" came an old gnarled voice in reply. "A visitor? How extraordinary," he went on.

"Err, Hi, we have come to see the Oracle," I said.

"Well, you had better come in then. Come on, come on," came the suddenly animated voice.

So in we strode, man and dog. The cave opened out into a vast chamber, with a blazing fire in the middle. There was a natural chimney in the rock above in which the smoke spiralled out. Flickering shadows played across the walls. At the back of the cave sat an old bearded man on a seat carved out of stone. He had long white robes with a white beard to match. His eyes were the most mysterious thing about him; the orbs burned like hot coals in a fire.

"Err ... are you the Oracle?" I asked tentatively.

"Not very sure of yourself are you sonny," replied the old man. "I have many names, but Oracle is one of them, yes."

"Can you help us please?"

"Well that depends on what you class as help?"

"Do you always answer a question with a question?" I asked.

"That depends what the question is?"

I could see that this conversation was going nowhere quickly.

"Sit down," the Oracle beckoned to a stone carved seat opposite him.

I quickly took the seat and Trinity lay down at my feet.

"Now, what have you come to ask?" enquired the Oracle.

I explained that we were lost and that we had travelled over from what has been called the mortal world into this twilight world and were looking for a way back.

"You are not lost dear friends, you are found," the Oracle replied cryptically.

"No, we are definitely lost," I emphasised.

"You are definitely found," replied the Oracle annoyingly.

I could see that conversations with the Oracle were going to be very frustrating.

"How are we found?" I asked.

"Ah, in your story, you mentioned a red stag. The red stag found you and brought you here for a purpose."

"Exactly what purpose would that be then?"

"To put right the wrong of course and restore balance."

"What wrong, what balance?" I asked.

"The wrong of mankind and the balance of the twilight moon."

This was all very cryptic and not making much sense to me.

"What is the wrong that mankind has done?" I asked, "And how do I balance the twilight moon?"

"Mankind has damaged something from this realm and only mankind can repair it. The twilight moon must be made three; for three is the order of the realm."

"Don't you ever give straight answers?" I queried.

"No self-respecting Oracle tells all; it is up to the adventurer to find what the Oracle can't reveal."

"Can you not tell us the way back?"

"The way back is forward and only by succeeding in your purpose will you be able to return home."

"OK, where must I go to repair the damage made by mankind?"

"I thought you would never ask. Journey onwards across the Lake of a Thousand Souls to the Shores of Abandon. Cross the Desert of Bones to the Crystal Forest. There find the fractured skull; the rest is up to you. That is all I will say."

"What is this fractured skull and how do we cross the Desert of Bones?" I asked forlornly.

But the Oracle was no longer speaking. He had closed his eyes and now sat snoring on his stone seat.

"I guess the audience is over," I sighed, looking down at Trinity. Trinity, as is her custom when her master is exasperated, rolled her big brown eyes.

Right, so we had to journey onwards across the lake. There was just one problem though; how were we to get back down the mountain?

I explored the cave with Trinity, not sure what I expected to find; a lift perhaps? There was no lift but there was a waterway at the back of the cave, assumedly where the Oracle got his water from. This sloped gently downwards then disappeared into a passage through the mountain. There was a chance, I thought, that we could follow this back down the mountain. Seeing no other option I grabbed a torch from one of the walls and beckoned Trinity to follow. I stepped into the water and Trinity, thinking that I was playing, came bounding after me. The next thing I knew Trinity had bowled me over and I was sliding face first down the waterway with a cute three-legged dog on my back!

"Whoa!" was my last word before we disappeared into the blackness beyond. We got tossed around, as if on a waterslide in a theme park, with no idea of where we were going; hoping against hope that we wouldn't be crushed against a rock face or flung off a massive drop. As it turned out we were flung off a massive drop, as the water exited the side of the mountain in a waterfall. We fell some 100 feet into a deep pool of water below and managed to surface coughing and spluttering. By some miracle, we survived the drop intact. Great, so far so good, but where were we now?

As it turned out, the only exit from the pool was another waterfall; sheer cliffs surrounded the rest of the pool. Oh great, I thought. Still, in for a penny, in for a pound; I decided on our only exit. This time, however, I pushed Trinity first, knowing she wouldn't go on her own. I followed straight after her.

Another 100 feet below we splashed down again, once more remarkably surviving intact. So what now? As it happened it was more water, followed by lots of air time, followed by more water. Our way down the mountain was by a series of slides, leaps, yelps, cries and splashes.

It was a rather battered and bedraggled pair that eventually made our way back to the turtle on the beach. All the turtle had to say was: "So you found the Oracle then."

Chapter 6 – The Shores of Abandon and the Desert of Bones

I described to the turtle our little adventure and asked him if he knew of the Shores of Abandon. A dark look passed across the turtle's wizened face as he replied: "The Shores of Abandon are the most desolate place in the Twilight Woods; in fact the only place more desolate is the Desert of Bones, but you wouldn't want to go there."

"Oh, great!" I said.

"Oh no," replied the turtle, "you do want to go there!"

Once more we climbed up the turtle's grassy back and set off on the lake for the Shores of Abandon.

Having wrestled with the spirits of the lost souls on the way, the journey across the lake to the Shores of Abandon was without incident. The shores themselves were another thing altogether though.

It was hard to see the shores at first, for they were black against the black water of the lake. As we got nearer though we could see the black sand that stretched as far as the eye could see, dotted with white skeletal trees on which jet black ravens perched. Ravens also circled overhead. The turtle swam up to the shore and started the long journey across the black sand.

The eternal twilight didn't help with the atmosphere, making the trees and ravens have a spectral blue glow. The further we went into the beach the more the ravens circled, knowing that many a poor soul got lost and died here.

Soon we lost sight of the lake and all that stretched in every direction was the black sand. The turtle stopped, unsure of the way. I looked to the moon, which hung on the horizon and said, "Head towards the moon, it is our only hope."

We followed that lunar highway of light for what seemed an eternity, always keeping the moon straight ahead, until eventually the sand changed from black to white and we knew we were on the edge of the Desert of Bones.

Tentatively I asked the turtle, "Why is it called the Desert of Bones?"

"Look and you shall see," came the reply.

I looked and what at first I thought was dead trees and vegetation, turned out to be bones and skeletons of all manner of creature.

"It is said," continued the turtle, "to venture into the Desert of Bones is to die."

"Can we go round it?" I asked, somewhat hopefully.

"No, it stretches too far in either direction; the only way is to cross it. Let's hope the ravens don't get a feast this twilight moon!"

"Onwards it is then," I said with more conviction than I felt, "keep heading towards the moon."

"Look out for quicksand," replied the turtle, "where there are bones, there is usually quicksand nearby. Steer a wide course around the bones, or be sunk forever in a sandy pit of doom."

I took my lookout position on top of the turtle and shouted commands, left or right, giving a wide berth to all the bones. This worked fine, until we crested a ridge and came to a valley with a wall of bones lining the bottom. The bones stretched in either direction for as far as the eye could see. There was no way past; what were we going to do now?

I commanded the turtle to stop and surveyed the scene. The slope down to the valley was very steep and it would be hard to control any descent. Even if we were able to stop at the bottom, there was no way through the bones. I looked left and right down the valley walls and could just make out a rocky outcrop three quarters of the way down the slope. I had an idea, but I wanted a closer look before I shared it with the turtle.

"Can you move along the ridge to the left please," I asked the turtle.

"Of course, but I am not sure how it will help"

When we were above the rocky outcrop I commanded the turtle to stop again. The slope was steep and slippery with moving sand down to the outcrop; there was no way we could stop if we went down there. A sandy ridge formed on top of the outcrop, which was just what I wanted.

"I have an idea," I said.

"Go on," replied the turtle.

"If you tuck your flippers in, do you think you will slide fast down that slope?"

"Too fast to bear thinking about," the turtle responded.

"Good, now what would happen when we hit that ridge on the outcrop down there?" I asked innocently.

"What!" cried the turtle?

"We would become airborne in a big way," he continued.

"And do you think we would clear the wall of bones?"

"Well yes, we might, but surely there is a safer way?"

"It's either that, or sink in the quicksand at the bottom."

"Hmmm ... I'm not sure."

I waited.

"Ok, I suppose, but it could be a tricky landing. We turtles aren't built to be airborne you know. Aerodynamics aren't our thing."

"I'm sure you can do it," I encouraged him.

"Come on, it's now or never!"

"Ok, here we go, hold on tight."

I lay flat on the turtle's back and gripped Trinity tightly. Then with a surge, the turtle pushed off. As soon as we crested the ridge and headed down slope we picked up speed straight away. Faster and faster we went, the wind and g-force trying to push us off. Turtles' shells must be pretty smooth underneath and built perfectly for sand sliding. I saw the sand ridge coming towards us at an alarming rate. 'This is it', I thought, 'We are going to crash and die'. The next thing I knew we were airborne.

"Whoaaaa ..." I cried.

We flew through the air like a missile and stayed airborne for three or four seconds. Then we landed with a thump, throwing Trinity and I into the air, landing in the sand in a heap. We were winded, but ok. I looked to check how the turtle was and saw him extracting himself from the sand. When he emerged he shook himself off and said, "It's going to take me ages to clear my shell of sand."

"We did it!" I cried

"We did it," the turtle reluctantly agreed.

The rest of the journey across the Desert of Bones passed without incident, with the piles of bones and quicksand appearing less and less often. Towards the end of our trek across the desert we saw a blue light shimmering on the horizon, like thousands of bright blue fairy lights. As we got nearer we could make out that these were crystal trees, refracting the blue twilight light and sparkling; we had reached the crystal forest.

Chapter 6 – Crystal Forest

As we entered the crystal forest, the trees dispersed the blue twilight light from their branches in kaleidoscopic patterns that danced over us. When the wind blew their crystal leaves made beautiful ringing sounds, like thousands of tiny bells. We stood mesmerized by the sound and light show that had greeted us. But where do we go now and what of the fractured skull?

"I must leave you here my friends, for the paths through the crystal trees are too narrow for one such as me. Go safely and keep following the moon."

"Thank you turtle, we would never have made it this far without you and owe you our lives," I replied.

"It is you two who should be thanked, who have been dragged from your home world and for what you are going to do to heal this world. Take care as you journey on; I hope we meet again. Now go, follow the moon."

With that the turtle turned around and made its way from the crystal forest.

I stood there for a moment and wondered at the weirdness of everything. Was I really going insane? How could there be a giant turtle with a carpet of flowers on its back behind us and a vast crystal forest ahead of us? Were these delusions? I didn't know the answer and tried to put it out of my mind for the time being.

The moon shone through the trees in a river of silvery blue light. Quickly we followed that passage of light, underneath a canopy of crystal branches shimmering in the moonlight.

The play of light through the trees and the ringing of the leaves was almost hypnotic, making us feel relaxed and at peace with the world. This peace was shattered, literally, by the sound of smashing glass. I looked around to see where it had come from, but could not spot anything and so kept going. Again the sound of smashing glass could be heard, but this time it was much closer to us. I looked up and saw what looked like icicles hanging from the trees, but could see by the way the light was refracted through them that they were in fact glass. As I looked, one of the 'icicles' dropped from one of the branches, shattering into shards of razor sharp glass. These glass icicles could kill us, I thought alarmingly. The question was, how do we make our way through them safely?

As I stood there pondering our route, I saw the most extraordinary thing: What looked like a man made of glass. He was tall and thin, with a body made up of dozens of shards of glass. He walked with a staccato angular gait and was coming towards us.

In a voice like fractured bells he called a warning to us: "Get off the path of moonlight quickly ... now!" as another glass icicle crashed next to us.

Taking heed, we quickly moved away from the full glare of the moonbeam where the glass man quickly joined us.

"Hi, I am Splinter, guardian of the crystal woods. What brings you here?"

"Hi Splinter, I am Jake and this is Trinity. We came here in search of the fractured skull."

"You choose a dangerous time my friend, under a twilight moon. Only a twilight moon can melt the glassicles on these trees and if one hits a mortal, you are sure to die."

"Oh, that is why you warned us to get out of the path of the moonbeam then."

"Yes, it is. But you must still follow this path if you are to find the fractured skull. Only the twilight moon can lead you to the skull. I suggest, however, that for safety's sake you keep well to the side of the full beam as you follow the path."

"Thank you for your advice Splinter, but why are there such terrible things as glassicles in such a beautiful forest?"

"There didn't used to be, but since the skull became fractured a disease has spread through the forest; tainted glass spores have attached themselves to the trees and grown into these deadly glassicles. If you are seeking the fractured skull, you must repair it and then all the poison will be drawn out of our Twilight Realm."

"Repair it we shall, if we can find a way."

"Then I will help you and accompany you further through my crystal forest. Follow me, I will lead the way."

With that he turned and started walking in his scratchy, staccato, angular gait. Gesturing to Trinity, we quickly followed.

It was lucky that we had Splinter with us, for the way was strewn with all sorts of obstacles. First there was a glass hedge of thorns that blocked our way, but with a gesture from Splinter the hedge parted and let us through. Then there was a glass lake, which looked too thin to cross. This time a gesture from Splinter resulted in a series of glass plinths rising up through the lake and acting as stepping stones to cross. Trinity dutifully leapt into my arms whilst we crossed. Next came the glass chasm, which was too wide and deep to jump. Unfortunately, this time, Splinter didn't have a gesture and the hoped-for bridge didn't appear. We were stuck, at least for the time being.

"Any ideas?" I asked Splinter hopefully.

"I was rather hoping you might," responded Splinter.

I looked at a tree that was overhanging the chasm and had an idea. "I know you are not going to like this Splinter, but is there any way of cutting this tree down so that it falls across the chasm and makes a bridge?"

Splinter looked horrified.

"It's the only way," I urged, "It's for the good of the forest if we reach the fractured skull."

"I … I don't know …," replied Splinter, his voice trailing off nervously.

"Please," I begged and, as if to emphasize the fact, Trinity gave him one of her best sad looks.

"I … I suppose," stuttered Splinter, "but only for the good of the forest."

With these words Splinter went up to the tree and started sawing at the base with his hand.

"My hand has got a diamond edge," he explained, "which is good for cutting glass. I usually use if for pruning."

It was a long and arduous task, but eventually there came a sound of fracturing glass and the tree toppled over the chasm, with Splinter moving out of the way just in time.

We crossed over safely, with Splinter leading the way and me carrying Trinity.

On the other side, the trees gave out to crystal rocks; whilst shining brightly in the twilight moon ahead was a crystal mountain, emitting dazzling patterns of light over the surrounding plateau.

Splinter led the way to the foot of the mountain and stopped at an entrance to a mine. "Behold, the crystal mine. In the depths of the mine lies the fractured skull, but there are many dangers ahead. Are you prepared to follow me into the mine?"

"Yes," I said nervously. Trinity rolled her eyes.

Chapter 7 – The Crystal Mine

As we entered the crystal mine I noticed a green glow.

"What's that glow, I asked Splinter?"

"Phosphorescence," replied Splinter, "the crystal rocks have a material inside them that glows naturally in the dark."

We followed the tunnel down for quite some way, until we reached a fork in the passage.

"Which way now?" I asked.

"I don't know," replied Splinter, "Never been here before, never dared."
"Err, I don't suppose you have a map?"

"No."

Left to our own devices, we could have been considering which way for quite some time, but Trinity had other ideas. She was on the scent of something and sniffing at the ground she headed down the left hand passage.

"Follow Trinity," I said. And so we continued on our way.

As we approached a bend in the passage, I suddenly saw a flickering red light make its way across the wall.

"Scanner," hissed Splinter.

"What's a scanner?" I whispered.

"They are deadly creatures who scan these tunnels looking for life forms. If they detect you they fire beams of intense light at you that can fry you in seconds."

"Oh," I said, "Shall we take cover then?"

"What a good suggestion; lie flat on the ground."

Grabbing Trinity and lying her next to me, we took cover as the red beam came round the corner. The scanner hovered in the air; it was shaped like an eye with a red beam moving from side to side projecting out from the iris. The beam passed inches over our heads, but thankfully didn't go any lower. However, if the scanner came further down the passage, we were doomed for sure, because it would run into us. I took a crystal rock and tossed it underneath the scanner behind it. It spun round and zapped the rock with its beam, instantly vaporising it. This distraction seemed to work, for it kept going back that way in search of more targets to destroy. We were lucky this time, but I realised we might not be so lucky in the future.

"Is there any way of protecting ourselves against the scanner?" I asked.

"None that I know of," Splinter replied.

I couldn't help thinking that there must be. I thought about what I knew about lasers, which seemed very much like the scanner's death ray. I knew lasers could be reflected with mirrors, if only we had a mirror.

"Is there any way of making a mirror?" I asked Splinter.

"Mirrors? Well yes, if we can find a pool of quicksilver and I know there are quicksilver pools in this mine."

"Great, let us hope we find one soon, because I think I have a way of defeating these scanners if we can make a mirror big enough."

We set off again with Trinity leading the way, her nose to the ground, sniffing a scent only she could smell. At every junction Trinity quickly chose a turning, each turning leading us further down below the mountain. These passages must go down as far as the mountain goes up, I thought.

After a while, I heard the steady drip of what I thought was water ahead of us. It turned out to be quicksilver, leaking from a vein in the crystal rock and dripping into a pool.

"Quicksilver?" I queried, when we arrived at the pool.

"Quicksilver," confirmed Splinter.

"Just what we need," I replied, "Now how do we make a mirror?"

"That's easy, you just dip a bit of crystal rock into the pool and a layer of quicksilver will attach itself to it. The rock carries a faint electrostatic current that causes the quicksilver to adhere to it," Splinter explained.

"Can you cut us a large flat piece of rock about our height?" I asked.

"Yes, I can do that, no problem."

Splinter proceeded to cut out a large section of crystal rock from the wall with his diamond tipped hand. I then took the rock and dipped it in the pool. What emerged from the pool was a brilliant mirror. Having admired my handsome form in it I showed it to Splinter and Trinity. Trinity immediately tried to play with the dog behind the mirror, such was the clarity.

"Excellent, we have what we need to see off those scanners," I stated.
Which was good as it happened, because just then a red beam appeared round the corner.

Quickly I raised the mirror in front of me and gestured for the others to stay behind me. When the beam hit the mirror, it bounced back, momentarily confusing the scanner. The next thing it did was to fire its death ray at us, which was a big mistake, for it too bounced back and vaporised the scanner.

"Wow!" exclaimed Splinter, "That was brilliant."

"Woof" went Trinity, I think in agreement.

"Hey, I think we have ourselves a scanner shield," I said modestly.

Now that we had a scanner shield, we walked with more confidence and quickened up our pace. We encountered three more scanners as we kept descending further and further below the mountain, each one of them frying themselves in our mirror.

After we had defeated the third scanner, we came to a vast hall. It was a cathedral of light, with pillars and arches of crystal soaring up from the floor above us. In the centre of the hall though was something I never imagined I would ever see: it was a huge dragon made out of crystal. I doubted my mirror would have much effect on dragon flame and put it down.

Again, I started questioning my sanity. It was hard to believe that I was deep below a crystal mountain, in a crystal hall, with a crystal companion, about to face a crystal dragon. I wondered if this was my psychosis or if in fact I was dreaming it all. The immediate problem was that the dragon looked pretty real and it was stirring from sleep. In all the books I have read, it's never a good thing to wake a dragon.
Trinity barked, just to make sure though. Trinity is not much of a barking dog, but she certainly chooses her time to bark. The dragon awoke.

Its eyes were like fire, burning deep and bright. Its jaws were huge, set with razor sharp teeth each half the size of a man. When it spoke, it did so in a voice like a thousand windows smashing.

"Who dares disturb me in my slumber of ages?"

Noticing that Splinter had taken a step backwards, I decided it was me who was going to have to be spokesman. "Err ... just three travellers in search of the fractured skull." May as well get to the point, I thought.

"THE FRACTURED SKULL!" the dragon roared.

"Err ... yes." Perhaps that wasn't such a good idea, I decided.

"How dare you come skulking, trying to steal the fractured skull?"

"No, we have come on a mission to heal the fractured skull and with it the Twilight Moon."

"Hmm ... that's as maybe, but I am the guardian of the fractured skull and you will have to answer this riddle if you are to gain access to it."

"Why yes, if a riddle it must be, we will try and answer it."

"Of course, if you fail to answer it ..." The dragon gave a dramatic pause, "then I will eat you."

"Oh, perhaps there is some other way?"

"No, there is no other way and I am hungry after my long sleep. Now, for the riddle: Who fractured the skull?"

"That's not a riddle, that's a question. How am I supposed to know who fractured the skull, I've only just heard of it from the Oracle?"

"That meddlesome old man, trust him to send someone to wake me! Now come on, give me the answer to my riddle, I've gone a long time without eating and I am losing patience."

"Can I confer?"

"If you must!"

"Splinter," I whispered, "do you know who fractured the skull?"

"I don't know, I am afraid. All I know was that it was fractured by some evil force a long time ago."

I tried to think about what the Oracle had said and of all the evil that was in our world. But it was not our world, it was the twilight world. Then I had it!

"Mankind fractured the skull," I replied, more confidently then I felt.

"What! How did you know that? Have you cheated somehow?"

"I knew it because I have been sent to repair the damage of mankind. The fractured skull must have been damaged by mankind."

"Then repair it you must, but not even my fire is strong enough to repair the skull."

With that the dragon raised itself onto its feet, arching its mighty wings as it did so. Underneath one of its claws rested a crystal skull, with a fracture clearly visible running down the middle of it.

"Behold the skull, key to this world and many beyond. Take the skull and repair it if you can. But beware, if you fail, I will eat you."

Nervously I strode forward and reached for the skull under the dragon's right claw. As I was about to take it, the dragon leaned forward, its jaws inches from my face. "Remember, don't fail, you know the price!"

With that, he lifted his claw and I took the skull. The crystal was smoky inside and felt alive in my hands. Splinter looked at it and said "That's smoked quartz, very rare indeed. I have never seen a piece that size before; it is supposed to have special powers."

"But how am I supposed to repair it?" I asked.

"That I am afraid I can't tell you," Splinter replied, "but perhaps the Wizard of the Winds can."

Chapter 8 – The Valley of Doom

"How do we find the Wizard of the Winds?" I asked.

"That's easy, he lives on top of the highest mountain in the Twilight Realm, Mount Eerie. It's the steepest, darkest, most dangerous mountain of them all."

"Sounds lovely," I said with all sincerity.

"Oh and did I mention the snow beasts who are said to frequent its upper reaches?"

"No, but thanks for telling me anyway ... and where exactly is Mount Eerie?"

"It lies beyond the Valley of Doom."

"Somehow, I thought you were going to say something like that. You do have dramatic names for everything."

"It reflects the character of the places," Splinter replied apologetically.

"I could do with less character," I responded wearily.

The journey back up to the surface was less adventuresome; the scanners didn't bother us and there were less turns to make. It was still a long arduous journey and we were all exhausted and needed a rest when we finally emerged on the surface.

"We are on the other side of the crystal mountain to what we came in on," said Splinter. "The Valley of Doom lies just ahead of us."

"Err ... I don't suppose there is any other way of getting to Mount Eerie is there?"

"The valley is the only way I am afraid, unless you want to turn back of course?"

"Well, no, I keep getting told the only way back is forwards."

"Onwards it is then," said Splinter, as he strode out onto the path ahead.

Trinity and I followed, with me feeling slightly awkward carrying a crystal skull in one hand. I was getting that surreal feeling again, where I didn't know whether what I was experiencing was real or unreal? I still wasn't sure if it was my bipolar plaguing me and I was experiencing psychotic delusions. Quickly I tucked the crystal skull in my backpack; out of site is out of mind I thought. I could feel its smoky eyes staring at me from inside my backpack though, boring through me as if searching for my soul. I shuddered and carried on.

The path ahead started to rise sharply, winding its way into the foothills of a large mountain range that seemed to go on forever. Soon the valley sides formed steeply either side of us and we were led forwards in a kind of funnel.

Tentatively I asked, "Why is it called the Valley of Doom?"

"There are various hazards in the valley: rock slides, floods, avalanches ... oh and then there is the trolls. They don't take too kindly to visitors. Let's hope we don't come any trolls."

"Great!" I wished I'd never asked.

As if to emphasize Splinter's warnings a rock came tumbling down the slope in front of us, just missing us by a few feet.

"Wow that was close!" I exclaimed.

"Wait until you see a full rock slide," replied Splinter.

The path kept going upwards and the walls of the valley narrowed in, forming cliffs either side of us. The cliffs were dark and oppressive, making me want to turn back. I couldn't help feeling we were being watched, but could see nothing to evidence that. Trinity's hackles were up, however, which usually meant trouble ahead.

A haunting howl went up that echoed off all the cliffs around. This was followed by several hoots and howls. Trinity started barking, warning us of danger ahead.

I looked up and could see dark figures looking out from caves in the cliffs, then the rocks started coming down.

"Troll attack!" shouted Splinter, "take cover."

This was all well and good, but I couldn't see anywhere we could hide; we were wide open to the rocks raining down on us. Trinity suddenly darted off to the side. "Where has she gone?" I cried. I couldn't see at first. Then I saw a small opening in the cliff face and leapt through it, dragging Splinter with me, just as a huge rock came crashing down where we were stood. "Phew, that was close," I said.

"Too close," responded Splinter. Where now?"

Although there was light streaming in behind us, the passage ahead of us was only darkness. Still it was either that or back out and face certain death by the trolls. I gestured that we should go on, putting Trinity on her lead as I didn't want to lose her in the dark.

The darkness was oppressive and we had to feel our way along the passage, the walls seemingly closing in on us. Why did it have to be the dark? I hated the dark, I thought. My mind began to imagine all kind of things; creatures lurking ahead with fangs dripping, waiting for us to step into their clutches. A spider's web brushed my face, making me jump. "Urgh," I said out loud.

The passage seemed to go on forever and I began to lose track of time. I felt disconnected, like a lost soul, haunted, trying to find its body again. I think detaching myself from the situation was my way of dealing with it.

After what seemed like an age, we began to hear water. Then my mind took to new imaginings. I started to fear that the tunnel would be flooded and that we would all be drowned in that dark lonely place, unable to escape our watery fate. The water however was outside and a glimmer of light announced the end of our dark journey. When we emerged I felt like I had been reborn, passing out of mother nature's birth canal, into the twilight world beyond.

We stepped out onto a rocky ledge, high up above a fast running waterway. There was barely room to stand with two feet on the ledge, which was slippery with the spray from the water tumbling down below us.

"What do we do now?" I asked, as much to myself as to Splinter.

"We keep going upwards," replied Splinter, although I already knew what the answer would be.

Keeping Trinity on a short lead for safety and with our backs pressed against the cliff face behind us, we edged our way up. The journey along the ledge seemed interminable and all the time I envisaged slipping, or Trinity slipping, and falling to our deaths, dashed on the rocks below. Eventually we rounded a corner, where a bridge crossed the chasm to a much broader path on the other side.

We made our way to the bridge, only to realise as we approached it that it was out in the middle. The bridge was made of stone and it arched over the water, hundreds of feet below, but there was a huge gap in the middle; it was obvious that it had been a long time since anyone had come this way. What to do now? I was frustrated, every step of the way brought on new dangers; it was if we were being tested, only this time I couldn't see any solution to the problem facing us.

Forlorn, I sank back against the rock wishing I had never entered this strange world. That brought on new anxieties as I was still unsure if it was all in my mind and everything that I was experiencing was some huge psychotic episode. Depression washed over me and engulfed me in its dark grip. I sank into its clutches like embracing an old friend, but a friend full of malice.

Trinity, my ever faithful companion, came up and nudged me and put her head on my lap. She looked up at me with her big brown eyes as if she were saying, "Master, don't worry, I understand." I would have been still slumped there now in a pit of misery if it hadn't been for Trinity. It was her support that brought me out of it, determined to find a solution to our latest problem. One way or another, I was going to get us across that bridge and out of this forsaken valley to Mount Eerie.

Carefully, I turned over onto my front and leaned over the edge of the path looking down into the chasm below, to see if there was any way down and across. Vegetation clung to the rock face, including vines that hung like tendrils all along the chasm walls. I wondered about climbing down them, but this was pointless as the rushing water was too fast to cross and we would be ground to death against jagged rocks if we tried. Then I had an idea.

I took my trusty penknife from my pocket and cut one of the longer vines. Taking this vine, I returned to the others and explained my idea to Splinter.

"I have a plan. We need to take this vine and loop it over that tree branch over there," I explained, pointing to a tree that was overhanging the bridge. "Then we can secure it and use it to swing across the gap in the bridge. One of us will have to go first and then we can tie it around Trinity and swing her across from one to the other of us."

"You call that a plan?" queried an unsure Splinter.

"Unless you have a better one," I responded.

"Well no, but ..." Splinter was lost for words.

"Good, let's do it then," I said with more conviction than I felt.

The looping and securing of the rope turned out to be easier than expected, but when it came to swinging across, my brain was saying one thing, but my body was refusing to go. I thought of my beautiful wife at home and how determined I was to get back to her, and decided that I must go through with it.

Taking the rope in both hands, I stood on the edge of the bridge and swung out across the chasm. The branch bent alarmingly, but in a whoosh of wind I just made it to the other side, still holding the vine. I swung the vine back across to Splinter, who proceeded to tie it around a rather bemused looking Trinity.

"Ready, "I said.

"Ready," replied Splinter.

"Go!" I shouted, signalling for Splinter to swing Trinity across.

With a whoosh, Splinter swung a wriggling, kicking Trinity across the chasm into the safe arms of her master. Two across, one to go. I swung the rope back across to Splinter and signalled for him to go. Closing his crystal eyes he swung out; the branch by this time had had enough and with a massive crack broke in two. I just caught hold of Splinter's arm and dragged him to safety as the branch crashed into the rushing water below.

"Phew, that was close!" I exclaimed.

"Too close," replied a visibly shaken Splinter.

After taking a few minutes out to recover, we set off again on the broader pathway on the other side of the broken bridge. The path soon wound its way out of the chasm and up into the green foothills of a mountain.

We had made it out of the Valley of Doom and now ahead of us lay the foreboding peak of Mount Eerie. Dark clouds hung from its jagged peak, which stood menacing and defiant.

Chapter 9 – Mount Eerie

The lower slopes proved to be green and verdant, providing us with no problems on our initial ascent; soon, however, the slopes became steeper. The ascent quickly became harder and we had to stop for regular rests before carrying on. As we climbed higher still the slopes became rocky, causing us to slip at times and for me to have to lift Trinity over some of the bigger rocks. My worry was though that as we got near the top we would encounter snow and freezing conditions, and we were not dressed for such exposure. The trouble was, I didn't know what to do about this.

As if in response to my worries, I saw a mountain hut ahead of us with its chimney smoking. Perhaps whoever lived there may have something we could wear to protect us from the elements; it was already getting cold.

I started to wonder at the regularity of things appearing in this world, just when I needed them. Was this a symptom of psychosis? Was I conjuring these things in my mind?

Deciding to go on and face what was either real or unreal we approached the hut, cold and tired from our climb so far. Tentatively I knocked on the door, not knowing who or what to expect.

Nothing, just a long cold silence. I knocked again, this time louder.

The door swung open and an old bearded man in leather trousers and a red checked mountain shirt stood there.

"I can hear you sonny, you got to give an old man time to get to the door. Now what do you want?" retorted the old man grumpily, his chest puffed out and long bearded chin jutting out towards me.

"Err ... sorry to disturb you, but we just stopped to ask if you could give us any assistance in climbing this mountain. You see, we didn't know until recently that we were going to need to climb the mountain and we haven't got the right gear."

"I can see that ... what did you think you were doing, going out for a nice autumn stroll?"

I thought back to the start of all this and the fact that this was exactly what Trinity and I were actually doing, but how could I explain it all to the old man?

"It's a long story," I said.

"Hmm ... that's as might be, but you can't go climbing like that. Better come in I suppose. Come on, hurry up! Don't stand there all day!"

We didn't take much encouragement and all quickly piled in and found Trinity already there, lying in front of the old man's fire. Trinity is a heat seeking dog and had snuck past the old man to find the fire whilst we were all talking outside."

"Darn dog!" the old man snarled, "how did she get in here?"

"Sorry," I replied, looking at him apologetically. I must admit I said to myself, it was one cosy fire and the thought of curling up in front of it and watching the flames flicker was all too inviting.

"Coffee?" enquired the old man.

"Why yes, that would be great!" I replied. "I'm Joshua by the way," I said offering my hand.

"Misty," he replied, taking my hand with a granite-like grip. "Sometimes they call me Old Man Mountain, but you can call me Misty."

"And my name's Splinter," added Splinter, shaking Misty's hand, "but no coffee for me thanks, plays havoc with my crystal."

"Take a seat," Misty beckoned, as he poured me a coffee.

"Thanks," I said, sitting down and accepting the coffee.

"So, you say you have a story. I'm all ears," said Misty.

I told him the story of how we had arrived here and the adventures we had experienced so far. I finally told him about the fractured skull, which really grabbed his attention.

"Show me," he beckoned.

I gently got the crystal skull out of my rucksack and showed it him. It seemed to tingle as I held it.

"Can I hold it?" he asked.

"Well, yes," I replied, suddenly strangely reluctant to release it.

Gingerly I passed it over and to my surprise, he took it almost reverently.

"Well I never, the fractured skull; never thought I would hold it. There's more to this skull than you can possibly imagine."

With these words he held it above the fire. Smoke from the fire seemed to mingle with the smoky rock of the quartz skull. The smoke in the quartz started to make patterns; circles and spheres, spirals and ellipses. None of it made sense, but it was as if the skull was trying to come alive. The smoky patterns, however, kept breaking down every time they hit the fracture.

"You must repair it, for the good of the Twilight Realm," he said, leaning forward and gazing intently into my eyes.

"That's why we want to climb the mountain," I said, "to go and see the Wizard of the Winds and ask his advice."

"Good idea, but not in that gear!" He remarked, looking at me. I'll see what I can find. "Splinter, do you need anything?"

"No thank you Misty, the cold doesn't affect my crystal."

I was quickly kitted out in mountain furs by Misty, and he even had a matching set for Trinity, saying he used to have a dog that suffered from the cold in the mountains.

Having warmed ourselves through, we made our farewells and headed back out. Misty pointed out a mountain track to follow that we hadn't seen before and we set out upon it.

The track wound its way steeply up the mountain and it wasn't long before we hit the snowline. The snow creaked under my boots as we made our way through it. Trinity, warm in her coat, ploughed through it bravely.

Snow soon started falling on us, so that everything became white. White on white didn't make it easy to see the path, but Trinity took the lead and showed us the way ahead. The snow began to pile up either side of the path and we were soon enclosed on either side by walls of snow. Someone, or some creature had made this path and I was wary that it may have been the yetis that Splinter had mentioned.

Snow became heavier and the wind picked up, blowing the snow into our faces. I could feel our strength sapping. To make matters worse I could see giant footprints in the snow; there were definitely yeti around and I didn't want to be their supper.

Green eyes peered from the snow around us that must belong to the yeti; how I wondered, would we get past them?

Suddenly a group of three yeti appeared on the path in front of us, with shaggy white fur, green eyes and disturbingly large fangs. They stood about eight feet tall and we were obviously no match for them. This was the end of the adventure, I though. I am either going to die, or wake up from this dream or hallucination that I was having.

In panic, I reached into my rucksack and took out the fractured skull, fully intending to throw it at them. The reaction when I took out the skull, was not what I was expecting. The yeti suddenly stood back, their snarls turning to yelps of fear and bemusement.

The next thing they did totally took me by surprise; they knelt before me, as if in adoration of the skull.

"Humba, humba," they cried. I have no idea what that meant. The skull buzzed in my hands, like electricity was trying to flow through it. I couldn't help thinking that if this skull wasn't fractured, it would be communicating with them. Still, their reverence for it had stopped them from making supper out of us.

Turning, they beckoned us to follow. This we did, not wanting to anger them. They led us to some huge arched caves in the mountainside, with giant icicles hanging down from the lip of the cave.

We entered the cave and before we knew it we were surrounded by twenty or thirty yeti, but none of them touched us. This fractured skull obviously held some special power over them.

Their leader, or dominant male, came up to us. He was even bigger than the rest of them and towered over us at a full nine feet I estimated.

"You, bring the skull of light." He spoke in a guttural voice. "Praise be to the skull and the masters who carry it," he continued. "You must repair the skull before our world ends. We will help you; we are at your command skull bearer."

"Can you take us to the Wizard of the Winds?" I asked.

"Yes, we will bear you on this sledge of bones to he who commands the winds."

With that, they pulled up a sledge made of human bones and gestured for us to get on board. Despite the grisly aspect to it, we decided to mount the sledge.

Four of them then harnessed themselves to the sledge and started pulling us up the track. The wind and snow by now was howling and we realised that we wouldn't have made it on our own. The walls of snow grew higher and everything became white.

After what seemed like an age, we came at last to the peak. Here they stopped the sledge and beckoned for us to go on to the caves at the peak. Trinity led the way and, after an arduous climb for about half an hour, we entered the caves; the caves of wind that howled with haunting notes through them. We had made it.

Chapter 10 – The Wizard of the Winds

Before us stood the Wizard of the Winds, his midnight blue cloaks flapping in the wind. He had a long white beard, large hooked nose, bushy eyebrows and piercing blue eyes. His long mane of white hair was swept back in a pony tail, but he bore no pointy hat; apart from that he looked every bit the wizard.

"Welcome," he greeted us in a deep, but somehow whistling voice. "I am the Wizard of the Winds and you have journeyed far."

"We have indeed Mr Wizard! I am Joshua, this is Splinter and Trinity my dog. Err ... if you don't mind me asking, what happened to your hat?"

"It was a nuisance," the wizard replied, "kept blowing off, can only wear it as a bed cap now."

"I see, can you help us please?"

"You have come to ask me a question: How to repair the fractured skull, am I right?"

"Why yes, how do you know that?" I responded, amazed.

"The wind told me. The wind is the keeper of secrets and tells me many things."

"Does the wind know how to repair the fractured skull then?" I queried.

"It may, or it may not do, we will have to ask it. Do you have the skull?"

"Why yes - it is safe in my rucksack," I replied, reluctant to get it out.

"It has a hold on you I see. It does that with all who touch it, apart from its guardian of course, the crystal dragon. Could you get it out for me please, so I can have a look?"

For some reason, my mind wanted me to scream "no" and run back down the mountain. I battled with this impulse though and slowly reached into my rucksack and withdrew the skull.

The skull buzzed with electricity when I withdrew it and I could feel its eyes boring into me. Quickly I handed it to the wizard, before I changed my mind.

The wizard took the skull reverently. By the respect that everyone showed it, the skull was obviously a very special item indeed.

"Ah, the crystal skull," he said, holding it at arm's length and gazing into its eyes. "What power I hold in my hands now; the power to control the winds and reshape the Twilight Realm in my own fashion; the power to control other worlds and all the life upon them; the power to harness the stars and light up the universe ... such power, such fragile and damaged power and it could be all mine!"

I felt tension and anger building inside me. He was trying to steal my skull from me and take it from its rightful owner.

"The temptation is strong," the wizard said, "but I know that if I use this power for myself, it will corrupt me and destroy all that I touch. No, I shall not take this skull for my own use, but it must be repaired in order for our world to heal. Take it back before I change my mind and come with me to the chamber of the four winds," the wizard beckoned, handing me back the fractured skull.

I snatched the skull back, loathing the power it was exerting over me, holding it with both hands close to my chest and followed the wizard to the back of the cave. Here was a staircase, which we climbed, spiralling round and around, higher and higher. By the time we reached the top we were quite exhausted and we staggered into a chamber that must have been right at the apex of the mountain. On each of four sides there were round openings through which the wind came howling, merging in the middle of the chamber to form a vortex. Underneath where the vortex formed was a large stone mouth with lips pursed, as if blowing.

"Place the skull on the lips," commanded the wizard.

Fighting the urge to return the skull to the safety of my rucksack, I took the skull and pushed through the wind to where the lips were. I then carefully place the skull on the lips.

What happened next, amazed me. The skull lifted off the lips, as if the lips were blowing it up and sat spinning in mid air in the vortex of wind. The skull itself then started flickering into life, with blue sparks of electricity shooting through it.

The wizard then raised his arms and seemed to grow even higher than his already tall form and spoke directly to the skull.

"May the four winds bless you; may the north wind give you life; may the south wind give you knowledge; may the east wind give you promise; may the west wind be your voice," he chanted, repeating it again and again, louder and louder.

Then, all of a sudden, there was a violent blue flash down the crack of the skull and the skull started speaking in a broken voice as old as time.

"I was formed before the first stars were born in the cauldron of the universe. I am all and I am nothing. I was broken by mankind when he used me for evil. Now I must be re-forged and made whole again. Seek the Cauldron of Life; only there is the flame hot enough to heal my fracture and make me whole once more."

With that the electricity stopped flickering inside the skull and skull was silent.

"Take the skull," the wizard beckoned. "It has told its tale and will speak no more."

I reached out and gently took the skull from the spinning vortex, returning it to my rucksack. I then asked the wizard, "What of this Cauldron of Life? Do you know what it is and how we are to find it?"

"The Cauldron of Life is older than the twilight world and the worlds beyond; it is more ancient than time itself. I don't know what or where it is, but the best place to start looking would be the oldest city in the Twilight Realm, which is beneath the sea. Seek the cauldron in the City of Shells; it lies deep below the Ocean of Light to the south of the realm. Now follow me; I will show you a speedy way down the mountain that will set you on the right course for the southern shores."

Chapter 11 – River Journey

We followed the wizard who took us down through a series of tunnels to an arched opening in the side of the mountain. Snow was still falling outside and it was very icy.

The wizard then pointed to a large sledge that rested just outside the cave. Take this sledge and follow the ice run down the mountain. It will lead you to the edge of a river, which if you follow it south eventually leads to the Ocean of Light.

I looked at the sledge and the steep icy run below nervously and asked, "Is it safe?"

"Fairly," replied the wizard uncertainly, "it always scares the hebejeebes out of me!"

"Great," I said.

Not wanting to climb back down the mountain, however, I reluctantly decided to follow the wizard's advice and climbed into the sledge, beckoning to Trinity to jump on board between my legs, with Splinter sitting behind me.

"Right, now take up the reins and I will push you. Try and steer as best you can."

"Right-ho," I responded.

"Ready?" queried the wizard.

"Ready," I replied, resigned to my fate.

"Here goes." With that the wizard started pushing us and all of a sudden, with a whoosh, we were on the run.

The speed picked up at an alarming pace, with walls of ice and snow rushing past us on either side. Yet still it went faster, until the walls became a blur and we clung on for dear life. A corner came looming ahead and frantically I steered to the right, just in time, as we rounded the bend. As we exited the bend the speed picked up even more; I couldn't believe how fast we were going. The wizard must be one hell of a speed freak, I thought. Another corner came into view; this time I steered left, running high up the curb. This was followed by a series of zigzag bends, which by a miracle I managed to steer through.

What came at us next was the mother of all corners. A huge wall of ice loomed up in front us, swinging round to the left, with a massive overhang on it. We hit the corner before I had time to steer and shot up to the top of the curb. Unable to stop, we flipped over and kept rotating until we came back down the other side. We had done an entire summersault and somehow survived and were now on a straight stretch again. There were several more twists and turns, exerting tremendous g-force before the end, but we managed to get through them more by luck than judgement. Finally we shot out from a long straight over a lip of ice and snow and flew into a big heap of powder snow. It was like landing in a giant bed of feathers, and although we all fell off in a heap we walked out unscathed.

Emerging from the snow we brushed - or in Trinity's case shook -ourselves down. We followed a footpath downwards, which took us through the final snowfields, until we passed the snowline and were back on green grass. The walking from here became easier and the path soon led us to the banks of a fast flowing river. This meant we were on course and just had to follow the river to where it emerges in the Ocean of Light. How far that journey would be we did not know. The long journey we had had so far was taking its toll and we needed a rest.

We trudged on for miles, scrambling down steep rocky patches that the river cut through in a rush of tumbling water. We came to a calmer stretch and saw a man out fishing in a boat.

"Ahoy there," I called, in my best nautical voice.

"Hello," the fisherman called back, "what brings such a strange party to these parts?" he continued, looking us up and down.

I suddenly realised what an odd party we must appear to passers-by; a man and a three-legged dog in furs, accompanied by a crystal man. Again I was set to wondering if any of this was real, or if I was hallucinating as a symptom of my bipolar?

"We have travelled far and are on our way to the Ocean of Light," I said.

"That sure is a long way to go on foot," the fisherman replied, "but perhaps I can help you. I am done fishing in these waters; there are very few fish around at the moment and I am heading down to the Ocean of Light myself. If you wish, you can help me crew the boat and travel with me?"

We considered his kind offer for all of a micro second; in our exhausted state sitting in a boat was a dream come true.

"Yes," I replied, delighted.

With that, the fisherman rowed up to the shore and flung out a rope for us to grab. I caught hold of it and pulled the boat up onto the river bank.

"All aboard, who's coming aboard," he shouted jovially. Trinity, not one to miss an opportunity, had already splashed her way up to the side of the boat and jumped in. She then proceeded to shake herself off, thoroughly soaking the fisherman.

"Sorry," I said, apologetically, not for the first time on this journey. Splinter and I then followed Trinity onboard, climbing in carefully.

The boat was a beautiful aquamarine in colour with one mast, which didn't have a sail hoisted on it at the moment.

"Mick," said the fisherman, by way of an introduction, holding out his hand. "Some people call me Mick the Fish."

"Joshua, "I replied, taking his hand, and this is Trinity.

"Splinter," said Splinter, also shaking Mick's hand.

"Right then me hearties," said Mick in proper seafaring jargon, "Let's push off and head downstream. Jack, you take an oar will you? And man the starboard side. I'll take the other oar and take the port side. When I shout 'Starboard oar' start paddling to starboard as quickly as you can; there are some pretty fast rapids out there and you need to have your wits about you.

"Aye aye captain," I replied, getting into the seafaring lingo myself.

"Off we go then," Mick said and with that he pushed off and we started heading downstream.

The first few hundred metres were fine, but then we came to our first rapids. I could feel the water rushing under the boat and rocking us from side to side. Quickly the right hand bank came towards us.

"Starboard oar," came Mick's command.

I was already starting to paddle as he said it and only just steered us away from the bank in time. Mick then started paddling frantically on the port side, just keeping us clear of some sharp rocks on the left bank. We then rocketed down some rapids, shooting in-between two rocks and out once more into clear water; this sure wasn't going to be an easy trip.

I was just starting to relax again when the current picked up and we rushed into the next set of rapids. This time the commands were quicker.

"Starboard oar," followed by "Full speed ahead", followed by "Starboard oar," again.

We zigzagged through a seemingly never ending stream of rapids with rocks high up on either side, waiting to smash our boat to pieces. Several times the boat scraped against the rocks, only fractionally avoiding being dashed against them and still the rapids went on.

Ahead of us loomed a whirlpool swirling round in a big funnel of water. I could feel us being dragged in.

"Paddle for all you're worth!" yelled Mick.

Too exhausted to answer, I put all my energy into paddling. Frantically paddling we swung around the lip of the whirlpool and with a surge of acceleration we slingshot out of it again. However, this sent us on a course for the rocks on the port side. Just as I thought we were going to get smashed to smithereens on the rocks, Mick brought us round, the side of the boat scraping against the rocks.

"Phew!" I cried.

"Rocks ahead," responded Mick. Straight ahead of us loomed two large rocks in the middle of the river, with water churning all around them. This is it, I thought, we are going to die.

Mick had other ideas though and with a superhuman effort he paddled for all he was worth, steering us just to the right of the rocks.

"Starboard oars," he shouted. Quickly I paddled with all my strength and kept us from crashing into the rocks on the right hand bank, sending us down a gully of water dashing through a narrow gap in the river's banks. We emerged from this, pulses racing and with great relief, into calmer water again.

"That was close," shouted Mick, "good job we had you on board Joshua."

"Thanks Mick, but I don't think I would like to try that again though," I responded.

"Don't worry you won't have to, we've made it through the gnashers; it's all plain sailing from here."

"How come you didn't tell us about the gnashers before we boarded?" I asked.

"Do you think I am daft? There is no way a bunch of land lubbers like you would have boarded if you had known, and I needed an extra oarsman," he said, with a twinkle in his eye. "Now let's set sail."

He hoisted the sail and the southerly breeze soon had us skimming through the water as the river widened out.

As the mountain receded into the distance, the weather improved; the twilight sky once more becoming cloudless.

The further south we went, the warmer the air became. The grass became yellower all around and we could hear crickets chirping. We were definitely heading into a warmer climate as we approached the Ocean of Light.

We passed many settlements along the river, some small villages, but also some larger towns. It was the first peaceful stretch of the journey and we got time to sleep, eat and rest.

The sound of seagulls announced our approach to the Ocean of Light, by which time we were well rested. Our first view of the ocean as we headed out of the estuary towards the sea was quite astounding; we realised why the ocean was called the Ocean of light.

Before us was a vast ocean that disappeared over the horizon. It was not the vastness of it that was astonishing, for all oceans are vast; it was the light emanating from it. A swirling fusion of light, in a myriad of colours, made the ocean glow, filtering up out of the water and dancing in rainbow waves of light across the twilight sky. It was a natural light show on a vast scale; a kaleidoscopic display of colour stitched into the twilight sky.

Chapter 12 – Underwater Journey

"Wow!" I said, my jaw dropping open, "What makes the ocean glow with all those colours?" I asked.

"It's the phosphorescence given off by natural plankton that the glow whales feed off here."

"It's beautiful," I said, "Do you know where the City of Shells is?"

"The City of Shells," answered Mick, startled. "That's nothing but a legend, a story told to children about a magical city under the sea."

"I am told it exists," I responded, "but I have no idea how to get there."

"I suppose that it is about as unlikely as coming across a man, a three-legged dog and a crystal man half way up a mountain," Mick said reflectively. "That said, I still don't believe it exists."

"Well I do," I said, with more conviction than I felt, for I didn't know for sure what was real and what wasn't anymore. This latest fantastical multi-coloured ocean of light made me question my perception of reality even more, and my sanity still further. Was I just imagining all this? Was my bipolar conjuring all these images from the twilight world? What world was I in at the moment? I didn't have the answers to these questions and so I ran with what I perceived to be the world currently and chose to pursue my quest for the City of Shells.

"Well, if you insist on pursuing this foolhardy journey to try and find the City of Shells, you will need a submarine. I know a man who has one in the local port, the City of Light. We will set sail for her now."

The City of Light was just along the coast from where we were. The port was a natural harbour in the cliffs where the houses were painted the same multi-coloured hues as the sky, which seemed to tumble down into the water from the cliffs above. It was beautiful and deserved its position on the Ocean of Light, complementing the ocean in its tumbling coloured architecture.

As we cut through the water across the port, the light swirled around the boughs creating rainbow patterns in the water. It was beautiful sailing on such a mesmeric light display.

We docked on a wooden quay and tied the boat to a post. Mick then took us round to the other side of the harbour where a large wooden boathouse lay. Wasting no time, Mick went up to a door in the side of the boathouse and knocked loudly.

"Jack, are you in there? I've brought some friends to see you."

"Mick, is that you? Well I never," came a voice from behind the door, which quickly swung open on creaky hinges.

"Hi Mick," said a beaming face in the open doorway, "what brings you here?"

"I've brought some friends to see you Jack; you'll never guess where they want to go. Darn crazy idea if you ask me."

I stepped forward and introduced myself, "Hi, I'm Joshua and this is Trinity."

"And I'm Splinter," added Splinter.

"Good to meet you all. So where is it that you want to go? It wouldn't have something to do with my sub by any chance?"

I recounted our story so far, concluding with "So that brings us to you; we need to find the City of Shells and with it being under water we wondered if you could help us find it in your sub."

"I told you it was a crazy idea," said Mick.

"Crazy it might be," replied Jack, "but recently I have been finding things on the ocean floor that just don't belong there. Items made out of shells, of kinds all things. You may think old Jack is going mad, but I am willing to go looking for this lost City of Shells."

"Nobody's as mad as Mick the Fish," replied Mick, "and if you are going on this crazy hunt for a lost city, than I'm coming along too."

"You'd all better come in then and I'll show you my sub."

We entered the boathouse and dominating the centre of the boathouse was a huge oval yellow sub.

"It's yellow," I stated, thinking of the Beatles' Yellow Submarine.

"Why yes," replied Jack, "all the best subs come in yellow - you can't go searching for a lost city in a grey sub, now can you!"

"Err ... I suppose not," I responded quizzically.

"Now, who's for coming onboard?" said Jack, as he walked across a gangplank to the sub's tower."

We followed Jack, who climbed a ladder on the tower and flipped open a hatch at the top. I passed Trinity up to him and climbed up after him. We then climbed down inside the sub, again passing Trinity between us.

Once inside, Jacked flipped a switch and warm yellow lights illuminated the inside of the sub. It was beautiful; brass pipes, whose function was beyond me, went up and down the length of the sub. Even the seats were brass with red leather trim. There was a series of six brass trimmed portals on either side of the sub, each with a seat for viewing. In the centre at the front was the periscope tube, again made out of brass. There was more brass in here than in the brass section of The Royal Philharmonic Orchestra, I thought.

"It sure is a beaut your sub," said Mick.

"Yes," I agreed, "Couldn't be a better vehicle for finding lost cities than this," I affirmed.

Jack looked pleased, like a proud parent. Then with the sound of a horn, he turned the engine on and set sail out of the boat house.

As we sailed out, I sat down at one of the portals and watched the rainbow hued water lap against the glass. It entranced me in waves of light and colour, soon sending me to sleep.

I awoke to the sound of Captain Jack sounding the horn again and yelling, "Dive! Dive! Dive! ..."

"Are we under attack?" I said blearily.

"No, but we have reached the spot where I found the shell artefacts and it is time to go down."

Jack started spinning a brass valve and there was a rush of water going through the brass pipes and filling the tanks of the sub. Soon the sub began to tilt downwards and make its way through the multicoloured water. Twin beams shone out from the front of the sub, cutting a path of light through the shimmering mix of coloured water ahead of us.

"We'll soon be below the phosphorescence layer of water and into the deep clear waters," Jack yelled over the rush of water.

"How far down do we go?" I asked.

"Thousands of leagues," replied Captain Jack.

As we entered the deep water, the surface colours dispersed; that is not to say that we were without colour, for shoals of brightly coloured fish swam past the portals. Shimmering jellyfish, glowing blue, also floated past. It was a beautiful marine world down below the surface, one that I felt privileged to see.

The further we dived the less marine life we saw, though, and the waters became darker and darker. I started to feel claustrophobic, trapped inside the metal shell of the sub, with the dark waters closing in around me.

Captain Jack immediately recognised this and said, "Don't worry, we all feel like this on our first deep dive. Take deep breaths and remember there is a vast amount of ocean out there and we are all here with you."

Jack makes a good captain, I thought. He could not only control the sub expertly but he had very good people skills too.

Still, as the water got darker and darker outside, with it my thoughts turned darker. The weight of the water mirrored the weight on my mind. I began to feel depressed. I was now desperately missing my wife at home and was worried that she herself would be worrying about me. I had become so self-absorbed in this anguish that I didn't hear the engines stop until Jack tapped me on the shoulder.

"We've reached the bottom," he said, "now let's use the searchlights to see if we can find some of those shell artefacts."

There were four search lights, one at the front of the sub, one at either side and one at the back. I manned the one on my side of the sub, controlled by a brass lever and started searching for anything unusual.

The light shone out across the sandy bottom, scattered with rocks, but nothing else. I looked out for what seemed like hours, without finding anything. Just as I was about to give in, I saw something white just peaking above the surface of the sand.

"Object to starboard," I cried, and was soon joined by Captain Jack.

I pointed out what I had seen to him and he was soon gently steering the sub over for a closer look.

"It sure looks like a shell object," said the Captain, it's a pity we can't go out and take a closer a look, but if we swam out at this depth the pressure would kill us.

"Not me," said Splinter, "I am made of Crystal, formed at high pressure. I should be able to swim out and retrieve the object.

Splinter equipped himself with breathing apparatus and left via the tower, which had a chamber that you closed to stop the water coming in.

He swam out following the beam of light from the searchlight that was now pinpointed on the shell object and was soon at his destination. Slowly he reached down and extracted the artefact and was soon swimming back with it.

When Splinter came back through the water chamber in the sub, we all gathered round him to have a look at the artefact. It was made of bleached white shell and had some strange markings on its surface.

"They look like compass points," said Mick, ever used to navigating.

"Yes, I would agree," said Captain Jack. "The one at the top must be north and there is one here with a line going through it; I think that must be a heading. That would make it south east I think."

"Do you think it is a pointer giving us the direction to the City of Shells?" I asked.

"It could be," replied Captain Jack, "I'll set a heading for south east and see what we find."

We chugged along for ages in a south easterly direction, but didn't find anything that remotely resembled the City of Shells.

"Are you sure it is this way?" asked Mick, "There is nothing but sand and rocks."

"Try a bit further," I said, more in hope, than expectancy.

After another hour a giant underwater mountain loomed up in front of us.

"I don't remember this on any charts," said Captain Jack.

"We have gone beyond the charts," replied Mick. "It's a mountain alright, but I see no sign of a city."

Meanwhile I was busy manning the searchlight at the front of the sub. "Wait, what's that?" I asked pointing to an opening in the rock.

"Some sort of passage I would think, but it would be foolhardy to go through there in a sub," said Mick.

"Speak for yourself," replied Jack, "I think I can get this sub into that passage safely. "Are you ready to try?" he asked his crew.

"Aye, aye captain," we all responded.

"Steady ahead then, here we go."

With that, Captain Jack slowed the engines down and set a course for the mountain passage. As we got nearer, the passage loomed large ahead of us. Soon we had passed the point of no return and we entered the passage. The darkness inside was all consuming and I could feel my claustrophobia returning. Captain Jack put a reassuring hand and my shoulder and whispered, "You'll be alright matey."

The searchlights highlighted the way; Captain Jack had to have his wits about him though, as there were several sharp twists and turns in the passage and one collision could fracture the hull.

Suddenly a wall of rock loomed head of us, with no obvious way round. A collision was inevitable and I braced myself for the crash and the watery fate that awaited me.

"Reverse engines," shouted Captain Jack and Mick slammed the engines into reverse. We slowed, but not enough I thought.

"More power to the engines," shouted Captain Jack and pulled a lever down that sent the engines screaming.

We were stopping, but would it be soon enough to avoid collision; I didn't think so.

We came to a stop just inches from the rock face.

"Phew," came the collective cry, but where were we to go now? The passage ahead was blocked.

"All this way for the passage to be blocked," Jack sighed.

"I knew it was a foolhardy idea," said Mick, "let's turn back."

"Wait," I said, "There must be a way through." Thinking quickly, "Is there any way of checking what is below us?" I asked.

"There's the observation hatch at the bottom of the sub," replied Jack, "let's have a look."

We gathered around the observation hatch, which was found in the engine room, and shone a light downwards.

"Nothing," I said.

"Then the passage continues downwards," replied Jack. "This will take some tricky manoeuvring, but I think I can take us down there."

Watching Captain Jack at the helm was to watch an expert submariner in action. His hands were a blur, pulling levers and spinning dials as he nudge the sub downwards. After a short while the passage levelled out again and we were heading forwards once more.

The passage had many more twists and turns, which Jack steered expertly through, but no more nasty surprises. We eventually emerged in a vast underwater lake.

"Up periscope," commanded Captain Jack.

Mick duly obliged, pushing the periscope up.

Jack peered through the periscope and gasped, "I think we have found the City of Shells," he said, offering me the periscope.

I looked through and was amazed to see a gleaming white city, with turrets and towers made out of shells. It sat on a white cliff, overlooking the lake and was a dazzling site to behold.

Chapter 13 – City of Shells

Even though we were in a vast cavern inside an underwater mountain, a twilight moon hung in the sky. I thought back to what the Oracle had said about the three moons: "The twilight moon must be made three; for three is the order of the realm." Perhaps this moon was the second of the three, with the first being in the Twilight Realm above? If so, where was the third?

"I think we should surface so we can be plainly seen. I don't think we should sneak up on the city, as that could be seen as furtive and perhaps even aggressive," said Mick.

"I agree," said Jack, "I'll bring her to the surface."

With that he started spinning valves, which made the brass pipes whoosh with the sound of ejecting water out of the tanks. Slowly we rose out of the water until the sub was sitting floating on the lake like a big yellow duck. It wasn't long until we were spotted and soon a flotilla of boats emerged from the harbour at the foot of the cliffs and came towards us.

Even the boats were made out of shells; huge shells for which I could only imagine what sea creatures used to reside in them.

The largest of these shell boats headed the flotilla and was soon in hailing distance of us. A tall man in white robes stood at the prow of the boat and spoke through a conch-like shell in a loud booming voice.

"Greetings travellers from the people of shells. We welcome you to our humble city beneath the mountain and beneath the sea. It is a long time since we have had visitors, cut off as we are from the rest of the twilight world. Long may the twilight moon shine on you and may peace be with you."

The silence that followed beckoned for an appropriate response. I turned to see everyone looking at me expectantly:

Captain Jack, Mick the Fish and even Trinity with her big saucer-like eyes.

"Ah, hem ..." I cleared my throat, "Greetings people of the shells, we have come a long way in search of your city and the ancient knowledge within. Please except us as your humble guests. Long may the twilight moon shine on you and may peace be with you."

"Welcome then friends; come follow us to the City of Shells."

By this time the boats had surrounded us and acted as our escort to the harbour beneath the City of Shells.

We arrived in the harbour to the cheers of the native population. We soon pulled up at a quay and as we stepped off the submarine we were greeted by beautiful maidens bearing garlands of shells, which they hung around our necks. Even Trinity was presented one, which she looked very pleased with.

"Thank you," I said, "your gifts are most wonderful. I am afraid we have no gifts to give you."

"Your gifts to us are your presence here," replied the tall man in the white robes. He was young and fair, with long blond hair flowing around his shoulders. I noticed that all the people here were fair skinned with blond hair. "Come," he beckoned, "follow me to the City of Shells."

We left the harbour, climbing up a staircase set in the cliffs. The steps were lined with mother of pearl and we noticed the cliff face was studded with white shells.

We emerged at the top of the cliff, through an arch made of whale bones, into a dazzling white square. The houses and shops lining the square were all made of white overlapping shells. Some of the buildings had spiral towers and chimneys made out of pointed shells; it was truly beautiful.

He led us to a magnificent building at the end of the square that was all turrets, towers and ramparts. "This is the city hall," he said, where we will have a feast to celebrate your arrival.

The inside of the city hall soared up above us, with a ceiling studded with shell mosaics of sea creatures and gods, supported on spiralling pillars of shells. We sat down at a table that ran the length of the hall, coated in mother of pearl; the seats were made of giant scallop shells.

A feast of exotic fish and seafood was laid before us, most of which I didn't recognise but all of which tasted delicious.

We were entertained by troubadours playing sweet music by blowing through a variety of shells with holes cut in them. They also sang songs of fair maidens and savage sea creatures.

When the feast had finished we retired to a smaller room set in one of the turrets. It was round, with views over the whole city and comfy seats at each of the windows to sit on.

"I am Rothfuss, Lord of the City and Keeper of the Shells," announced the white robed man.

We made our introductions.

"You have a story to tell, that I can see. Pray tell me what brings you to our humble city beneath the sea?" asked Rothfuss.

I retold our tale, which seemed all the more incredible in its retelling. Not for the first time I questioned the reality of it all, for here I was with an assortment of characters from another world in yet another world within that world. Could things get any stranger?

"And so," I said, "we found the fractured skull. The Wizard of the Winds sent us here, to the oldest city in the Twilight Realm, to seek the whereabouts of the Cauldron of Life in which to repair the skull."

"Quite some story young man ... and you say you are from another world?"

"Why yes, I am, it was a red stag who brought us here."

"Then the prophecy is true," stated Rothfuss, "that there will come a man from the world outside this world who will restore harmony to the three moons ...", he paused momentarily ... "Long ago our world sank beneath the Ocean of Light and we have been cut off from the Twilight Realm; it is our hope that through you we will find a way back."

"I am no magician," I said, "I am just a traveller seeking a way back. I am told not to go back, but that I must go forward. This means I must try and repair the fractured skull or else remain here forever. I don't know how to restore harmony to your world."

"Ah ... then we must help you on your quest to restore the fractured skull, for this is the key to it all. I believe if the fractured skull is repaired then harmony will follow. There is no Cauldron of Life here, however, but we have some ancient tomes in the library, which might be able to tell you where it is. Follow me, I will take you to the library."

The library, as it turned out, was deep beneath the city in catacombs built into the cliff. The catacombs had been hollowed out from shells and rock to make room for a massive library. We were met at the entrance by the librarian. She was beautiful, with gowns of the palest blue, almond eyes, cherry lips, a svelte figure and long blond hair down to her waist. I was instantly prepared to read any old book if this beautiful woman was to show me them.

"I am Cordelia, the Librarian," she announced, "what book is it you are seeking?"

Rothfuss explained we were looking for the oldest volumes, to try and find the location of the Cauldron of Life.

"Ah, then you will be wanting the Codex Historicus, an ancient history of the world," she said. "Come follow me." Which I did, without hesitation.

We went through passageways lined with books, until I had soon lost all sense of direction. We passed windows in the cliffs that looked out into the bay and cast light into the tunnels, the only light apart from candles burning in shell sconces in the walls.

Just when I thought that Cordelia herself was lost, she stopped in front of a large alcove with a locked door sealing it. Cordelia quickly unlocked the door with a chain of keys she was carrying. Then, carrying a candle, she beckoned us in.

There was a solitary desk in the chamber with one book lying upon it. "Here is the Codex Historicus; it must be handled very carefully. Now let me see, the Cauldron of Life you are looking for."

With that she began gently leafing through the huge volume until she stopped at a page and spoke: "Here it is, the only reference to the Cauldron." She began to read from the book: "The Cauldron of Life was taken by Master Smith to The Devil's Forge, there to forge the sword of truth ... the rest of the passage is obscured I am afraid."

"The Devil's Forge," I said, "then we must travel to The Devil's Forge. Does anyone know where it is?" Sounds a cheery place I thought.

Chapter 14 – Old Smoky

"The Devil's Forge lies deep below Old Smoky, an industrial city built on volcanic fields," replied Captain Jack. "We can go in the sub to the nearest town on the coast, Cold Wind Bay, and then get the steam train from there."

"Do you mind if I come with you?" asked Cordelia. "There is certain law I know about the fractured skull that might help and I want to help to re-establish a connection to our undersea realm again."

"Why certainly," I said, as the adopted leader, "If it is ok with Captain Jack, that is?"

"It will be an honour," said Captain Jack, with a twinkle in his eye.

The shell people were very reluctant for us to leave, as they hadn't had any contact with the outside world for thousands of years. They were particularly reluctant for Trinity to leave, as they had no dogs in the City of Shells and Trinity was an expert at making herself adorable; especially when there were plenty of fishy titbits on hand.

Eventually we managed to get away, with one slightly overweight sea dog. We were escorted back out with a flotilla of boats again before, with a blast of the sub's horn, we submerged and headed for the passage out.

The journey out was a lot easier than the journey in, as Captain Jack now knew all the twists and turns of the underwater passage and his expert hands steered us out with no problem. Once out we commenced the long journey to the surface during which Captain Jack, with the help of Cordelia, marked the position of the City of Shells on a sea chart.

Once at the surface we set a course due north for Cold Wind Bay. The journey was tranquil, with the coloured waters lapping at the sub mesmerizing us with their phosphorescent display.

We knew we were approaching Cold Wind Bay when a brisk wind began to pick up, howling around the sub's tower. I opened the hatch out of curiosity and stuck my head out and confirmed, yes, it was definitely a bitingly cold wind.

Cold Wind Bay soon appeared on the horizon with grey-black jagged granite cliffs forming the walls of the bay. We entered the bay to find a busy fishing port with fishing boats of all shapes and sizes sailing in and out of the bay. When we docked and opened the hatch a strong smell of fish assailed us, blowing in on the cold wind.

When we exited the sub, Mick the Fish was in his element talking to all the fisherman and spinning yarns about his fishing exploits. Before we left, Mick decided to stay and hire a boat to do some fishing. He promised that he would be there for us when we came back. I thanked Mick for all his help and we said our goodbyes.

And so it was that a party of five waited on the platform at Cold Wind Bay station for the Old Smoky Express. The express train when it arrived was enormous, far bigger than any train I had seen before. The engine was jet black with iron wheels the size of a house and stretching as long as a football field. The steam it gave out formed a cloud that entirely covered Cold Wind Bay. It was an industrial beast in every sense. We boarded one of the carriages, which was also black, and sat together in a compartment on cracked red leather seats.

"This train is huge," I commented.

"Aye, it is that," replied Jack, "it's built so big in order for it to be able to carry the vast quantities of iron ore they use in Old Smoky."

"Old Smoky must be one hell of an industrial city," I said.

"That it is Jack, wait until you see it!"

A whistle blew, that sounded like a thousand wailing banshees, signalling that we were off. The steam engine roared into life, emitted more steam than Yellowstone Park, and the train started moving. The train soon picked up speed and moved far quicker than any steam train I ever knew. In fact it was at least as fast as a modern electric express train, such was its enormous power.

The journey was spectacular, passing through high plateaus on which wild horses ran ringed by mountains that resembled many jagged teeth. We also passed large lakes on which pink flamingos fished. It was beautiful – well, at least until we reached the tunnel, then everything went black.

The blackness engulfed me, swallowing me in its inky grasp. I could hear the wind whistle off the side of the train and the chuff of the steam engine, but could see nothing; only blackness. I felt entrapped, like I was in a tomb. The sound of the steam sounded like some giant monster trying to eat me up. I went all cold and clammy, my heart started racing and I thought I was never going to get out of this blackness.

When we eventually emerged, after what seemed like an age, it was like being born again; passing out the darkness of the womb into the light of day.

Before long the mountains became black and black clouds filled the sky. The air felt grimy somehow. I looked at Jack, who nodded in recognition and said, "You can smell Old Smoky now; it gives off so much soot that you can smell it for hundreds of miles before you get there."

The nearer we got, the blacker the clouds became, until eventually we entered a black smog. Coughing, I enquired, "How can people live in this smog?"

"They get used to it," Jack replied, "although it's never pleasant."

Eventually, the city appeared on the horizon, framed by black mountains. The city was made up of tall grey skyscrapers that were covered in gritty grime from the smoke. Huge chimneys belched smoke and flames into the air; it had a brooding, almost menacing, feel to it.

We slowed down as we entered the city; huge towers and chimneys reached up into the murkiness above us. Fingers of light shone beams from windows and doorways through the grey smog as we passed by. The smoke was so thick that it coated the buildings in a black tar like substance.

We pulled in at an enormous station, vast black steel beams arched above us, whilst trains as big as ours steamed in and out of the station. A sign, partly obscured by grime said, "Welcome to Old Smoky."

"I can see why they call it Old Smoky," I said.

"Smoky by name, smoky by nature," replied Captain Jack.

"So how do we find The Devil's Forge?" I asked.

"That's easy," replied Jack, "we get ourselves some liquor."

"Err ... If you don't mind me asking, how is getting a drink going to help us find The Devil's Forge?"

"Barmen like to talk; if anyone is going to know how to find The Devil's Forge, it is going to be a barman. Now, there's a nice looking bar over there," Jack said, pointing to a bar with the uninviting name of "End of the Line."

"Looks like a cheery bar," I said sarcastically.

"Looks can be deceptive," replied Jack.

Jack, as it happened, turned out to be right. Inside, the bar was cheerily light, with wood and brass fittings. There was a bowl of water at the door, which Trinity was soon lapping away at, and a solid polished oak bar at which we all sat.

"Right, what's everyone having?" asked Jack.

I asked for a beer and Cordelia asked for a soda. Jack soon attracted the barman's attention and ordered our drinks, adding a whisky for himself. When the barman brought the drinks, Jack said, "and one for yourself."

"Don't mind if I do thank you," answered the barman, "I'll join you in a whisky."

Soon, we were drinking and talking to the barman.

"Jack," Jack announced, offering his hand to the barman. "My name's Billy," replied the barman, "Good to meet you," he said warmly, taking Jack's hand.

"This is Joshua and Cordelia, and the dog's name is Trinity," continued Jack.

We waved hello to Billy.

"Howdy," replied Billy.

"Now, Billy, would you happen to know how we find The Devil's Forge?" asked Jack, getting straight to the point.

"Hmm ... The Devil's Forge you be wanting; not many folk know where that is," replied Billy. "However, old Billy does! You're lucky you came across me. If you like, I can take you down there after closing time, if you don't mind sharing a few more whiskies with me," he continued.

"Don't mind if I do," answered Jack, "don't mind if I do."

Chapter 15 – The Devil's Forge

Aware that too much beer and I was not a good formula, I slowed down on my drinking. Jack and Billy however did not and by closing time, they were quite merry.

"Are you ready to show us the way to the forge?" I asked.

"Swhy ... yes, hic!" replied Billy, "I hope we don't fall in the laver flow though, itsssa bit hot I hear."

"Then sthere iss the tunnel beasts, not too friendly, or so I have sbeen told."

"Oh great, why is this world full of beasts and dangerous passages!" I exclaimed.

"Sssdon't blame me," slurred Billy, "You're the one who wants to find this cauldron."

"I just want to find my way home," I said, "but nobody wants to show me the way home. I have to keep going I am told and repair the fractured skull before I can go home."

"Sfractured skull is what I'll have in the morning," said Billy.

"Smeee too," agreed Captain Jack.

"I'm not bothered about your two noggins, it is the crystal skull we need to repair. Now can you lead us to The Devil's Forge please?"

"Salright, Salright, it's just down the hatch."

"You've done enough of that already!" I exclaimed.

"No, not down that hatch, down this hatch," said Billy, pointing to a hatch in the floor. Now slift it up and we will go and see if the devil is at his forge today."

I lifted the wooden hatch with a loud creak and a strong sulphurous smell wafted up through it.

"Swhoos farted," stuttered Captain Jack.

"Nobody's farted," I sighed, "Its coming from the passage beneath the hatch."

"Sthat will be the lava further down, stinks of sulphur you know," said Billy.

"Ok, let's go down," I said, "you lead the way Billy."

Again, I started wondering if this was all real. Here I was with two drunken adventurers, a beautiful librarian from an underwater city and a crystal man, about to brave lava flows and who knows what else? At least I had Trinity with me, my one connection to my own world; how I missed my wife and home. Would I ever return home or, worse still, was I already in my own world and all of this a delusion?

Billy staggered to the hatch and half climbed, half fell down the ladder leading down from the hatch. The rest of us followed, with Splinter and I passing Trinity between us.

The passage below was hot with an orangey red glow coming from the end, which was just enough to light the way. We made our way towards the fiery glow and were soon burning hot. I stripped down to my t-shirt, but was still way too hot. As we exited the first passage we could see the source of the light; it was a lava flow running across the passage with a small stone bridge across it. We crossed the bridge looking down on the slow moving lava with a black and red crust upon it, swirling and making patterns. Safely across we continued on our way, the passage fiery red from lava flows at either end.

We came to a junction with crossing lava flows and two bridges leading out over them.

"Ok Billy, which bridge do we take?" I asked.

"Sthat's easy, either the left or the right one I'd say," replied Billy helpfully.

"That narrows it down," I said.

"Sssok, the left then," said Billy.

"Are you sure?" I asked.

"Nope, but I don't like the look of the right one!" said Billy pointing.

I looked down the right passage and to my horror there was a couple of short hairy creatures running down it, about three foot high, but most of that three foot taken up with jaws of razor sharp teeth.

"Good choice," I said, leading the way over the bridge and down the left passage.

As we ran down the passage I looked back and, to my horror, the short hairy monsters were following us down the passage. We came to another junction with a stone bridge on the left and a wooden plank forming a bridge over the hot flowing lava on the right.

"Slets take the right bridge," said Captain Jack.

"Are you mad?" I asked.

"Strust me, I have an idea," replied Jack.

Wasting no more time we crossed the fragile right bridge, with Jack crossing last. When he was across, he quickly nudged the plank into the lava just as the monsters were going to cross. There was a lot of snarling and chomping, but they had no way of getting to us now. We, however, now had no way back. So onwards we went.

We adopted a left, right system of turns after that, taking alternate lefts and rights. We encountered no more monsters and kept going deeper and deeper below Old Smoky.

Eventually we exited out at a huge lava lake with lava dripping from the cavern's ceiling into the lake. We had reached a dead end with no way to cross.

"Where now?" I asked.

"Across the lake," replied Billy.

"Great, just one thing though, how do we cross the lake?"

"Sno idea," answered Billy, "but I do know that The Devil's Forge lies beyond the lake of fire."

"Wait," said a sharp eyed Cordelia, "can we cross on those stones over there?"

"Not stepping stones," I replied, remembering my earlier experience of crossing stepping stones, "I hate stepping stones."

"Have you any better ideas," she said, hands on hips.

"Well, not exactly, but does it have to be stepping stones?"

"Yes, it has to be I am afraid," Cordelia replied. "Now I am going to cross, anyone else coming?"

"Yesss ..." came the collective sigh of resignation.

Cordelia made the crossing look easy, but then she wasn't carrying a three-legged, now slightly overweight dog. There was no way I was going to let Trinity try and cross on her own.

I set foot on the first stepping stone, with Trinity in my arms and felt it sink a bit. The svelte Cordelia had run across without any noticeable shift in the rocks, but the combined weight of Trinity and I made them start to sink. I realised these stepping stones were actually rocks floating on the lava and as a result anything could happen.

I quickly stepped to the next stone before the rock sank completely, but the next rock started moving sideward as I stepped on it and I nearly missed it altogether. The stones were shifting all the time. I speedily moved to the next stone, which tilted alarming backwards and I had to leap, dog and all, to the following stone to avoid a fiery fate. There were only five more stones to go, I thought dismayed.

The first of the five stayed pretty much where it was supposed to be, but the next one rocked from side to side, making me step from foot to foot in order to keep my balance. I jumped to the preceding rock, only to be tilted forward at an alarming angle. Hastily I leapt to the next rock, which did the same. By now I was running at an almost horizontal angle. I just managed to keep my momentum going to the final rock before leaping for the shore on the other side, holding Trinity out before me for Cordelia to take. Cordelia managed to grab Trinity just in time, as I came crashing down onto the cavern floor. We had made it, but only just.

Splinter followed me in his staccato style, which seemed somehow oddly suited to the movements of the rocks and he made it across quite easily.

Captain Jack and Billy, still merry on drink, were next. It was quite comical to see the pair cross, swaying in opposite directions to the way the rocks tilted. It bore the resemblance of a drunken waltz. At one point they tilted into one another, bouncing apart again to continue safely. They miraculously made it across, despite the odds.

All safely across at the other side, we kept going forward until we reached the end of the cavern. Here we reached a dead end, for the only way out was through a fast moving lava flow going downwards.

"All this way to get stuck here," I sighed.

"There must be another way," Cordelia replied.

"Nope, this is the only way," said Billy, "Ssnow, I remember something about navigating the lava flow, ssnow, what was it?"

"Brilliant Billy!" said Captain Jack, somewhat over enthusiastically. "Navigating is what we will do; we just need to sail down the lava flow."

"Great," I said, "on what exactly?"

"On pumice rock," stated Splinter. "Pumice rock floats, as you have seen, and I think I can cut a piece big enough with my diamond tipped hand for us all to float down the lava on."

"Oh," I sighed. I was not sure floating down a red hot lava stream was my idea of sailing.

"Come on, let's do it!" urged Cordelia.

Not wanting to look a wimp in front of Cordelia, I replied, "Yes, let's do it, I'm not going to let that lava beat me."

Splinter quickly got to work cutting out some pumice stone and soon had a piece large enough for a raft cut and shaped.

"Ok, let's carry it over to the lava and then all scramble on board quickly," said Captain Jack.

So we carried it to the lava and Captain Jack leapt on to it first and shouted, "All aboard, who's coming aboard?"

We all scrambled aboard and the unlikely party of me, one three-legged dog, two drunkards, a pretty librarian and a crystal man started sailing on a stream of lava, destination unknown.

"Ssl christen this yacht The Phoenix," slurred Captain Jack.

"Let's hope she can fly us over this lava like a phoenix," I replied.

The makeshift raft quickly picked up speed and soon the rocky walls of the lava stream were whizzing past us. We had absolutely no control of the raft and just had to hang on for dear life. Lava dripped from the rocky ceiling above us, narrowly missing us on several occasions.

As we went down we were bumped against the sides of the lava stream, but thankfully stayed on course. That was at least until we heard the roar ahead of us.

"What's sssthat roar?" shouted Captain Jack.

"It can only be a lava fall," I replied, "like a waterfall, but in this case lava."

"Abandon ship!" yelled Captain Jack, waving his arms frantically.

"We can't," I shouted back, "there's lava all around."

"We need to steer for shore somehow," shouted Billy.

"Everyone get to the left hand side of the raft; that should lean the raft in the right direction. Quickly!" instructed a very level headed Cordelia.

Quickly we did as she said, but the lava fall was too near; we were almost certain to go over it.

"Lean to the left," shouted Cordelia, a hint of panic now evident in her voice.

We all put as much weight to the left as we could, but the shore wasn't coming quickly enough and the lava fall was looming.

Just as we were about to go over Cordelia shouted, "Jump for shore!"

We all jumped, my arms tightly wrapped around Trinity, and we only just made it, landing in a huge heap upon the shore's edge. I turned and watched the makeshift raft tumble over the lava fall into a burning pool of lava below.

"Phew, that was close," I said.

"Too close," agreed Splinter.

Together we looked down on the vast pool of lava, hissing and bubbling below.

"We've made it," said a now sober Billy, "This is The Devil's Forge."

"So where is the Cauldron of Life?" I asked.

"That I can't tell you," answered Billy.

Chapter 16 – The Cauldron of Life

"I remember something from the Codex Historicus," recalled Cordelia, "something about the Cauldron of Life can be found where the rivers of fire meet."

"That will be where two lava streams meet," I said.

"So all we have to do now is find out where two lava streams flow into each other," concurred Cordelia.

"I hate to say it," said Captain Jack, who had now also sobered up, "but I can see two lava streams flowing towards one another on the other side of the cavern, over The Devil's Forge."

"Great," I said, exasperated, "how the hell do we get there?"

"Where's Trinity?" I asked, looking around for her.

"I saw her sniffing her way across the side of the cavern over there," said Billy.

"Quick," I said worried, "let's find her." I had visions of her falling into The Devil's Cauldron.

We raced across to the side of the cavern, but could see no sign of her. My heart was in my mouth; what if she had fallen? It didn't bear thinking about.

"What's this?" said Cordelia.

We went over to where Cordelia was bent over looking at something. Low down in the rock face there was a gap. Trinity must have gone through there looking for mice or something.

"I'll have to crawl through," I said unenthusiastically, as I hated confined spaces.

Despite my claustrophobic fear my fear of losing Trinity was even worse, so I quickly found myself on my stomach crawling through and shouting "Trinity," as I went. I was soon in pitch blackness, so I had to feel my way along. I had an overwhelming feeling of the walls closing in on me, but still I kept going, banging my head as I went along. The ceiling was getting lower and lower, so I had to really flatten myself out as I crawled on. After a short while, however, red light began to illuminate the tunnel and I could see a red glow at the end of the passage. It wasn't long before I came out of the passage and into another part of The Devil's Forge cavern. Lying at the edge of the cavern was a very contented Trinity, who was loving the heat coming up from the lava. To my astonishment, though, in front of Trinity was a rope bridge stretching across The Devil's Forge. Somehow Trinity had found us a way across!

I went over and hugged Trinity, both out of relief and for finding us a way across. I then realised I had to make the journey back to get the others. This, as it happened, wasn't so bad, as I knew what lay ahead and soon found myself back with the others. I explained that Trinity was safe and excitedly described what she had accidentally discovered. I then led the way back into the tunnel. There was a lot of bumps and groans, but it wasn't long before we had all made it through the passage and back to Trinity. Now all we had to do was cross the rope bridge.

I looked across the bridge but noticed that several of the planks were missing; those that were still present appeared to be pretty rotten.

"Any volunteers for who goes first?" I asked hopefully.

The prolonged silence I took as a no. I hadn't taken into account Trinity though, who then decided to start making her way across.

"Trinity," I called, hoping she would turn around and come back.

The call was in vain though, as Trinity had adopted selective hearing mode and chose to not hear her master's command.

"Great," I sighed and followed Trinity across.

The bridge groaned and creaked as I stepped onto it. It accommodated Trinity's weight without any problem, but as soon as I added my extra weight to it, I felt it start to buckle. Still I had to follow Trinity as I was worried about her falling through the gaps between the loose planks.

I needn't have worried however, for Trinity was nimble enough, even on her three legs to cross safely and was soon on the other side. That left me in the middle of a creaking and groaning bridge. I was just wondering what to do when the plank underneath me snapped and I started falling. Luckily I managed to grab the ropes holding the bridge up just in time and was able to haul myself up onto the next plank. I decided that waiting wasn't an option after that and that speed was the best policy. I ran the rest of the way across hopping from plank to plank. Another plank gave way as I sprinted across, but my forward momentum got me onto the next plank safely. My plan worked and I was soon safely at the other side with Trinity, but we still needed to get the rest of the party across.

"Cross one at a time," I shouted, "the bridge will only hold one person at once."

From the expressions on the faces of the others, I didn't see much enthusiasm for crossing though.

"Who's coming across next?" I almost pleaded, not wanting Trinity and I to be separated from the rest of our group.

"I'll come, as I am the lightest," eventually replied Cordelia.

Not waiting another second, she started crossing. She didn't rush and the bridge was noticeably more forgiving with Cordelia's slight weight. Although it took some time, Cordelia eventually crossed without any incident and it was time for someone else to cross.

"I'll go next," said Splinter, buoyed by the success of Cordelia.

Splinter's crystal body was significantly heavier than Cordelia's, however, and when he started crossing the bridge creaked in protest straight away.

"Run," I shouted, "It's the best way."|

Wasting no time, Splinter started running in his disjointed, jerky way. This didn't have the effect I was hoping for as the very next plank gave way and he had to catch hold of the ropes to stop falling. Splinter somehow managed to drag himself onto the next plank, but stayed there, not knowing whether to cross or go back.

The bridge made its mind up for him, as it began to creak and groan ever more loudly under his crystal weight. Quickly splinter turned and sprinted back, just as the bridge finally gave way. Splinter leapt off the tumbling bridge towards the safety of the rocky ledge, as the bridge shattered and fell into the hissing lava below.

Jack and Billy, quick to react despite their thick heads, just managed to grab hold of Splinter and haul him to safety before he too joined the bridge in the bubbling lava below.

"That was a close shave," gasped Splinter.

"Too close," I said, "but now our party is separated."

"We'll wait here for you," said Jack. "You go on, it's important to find the cauldron and repair the crystal skull."

"But how will we get back?" I asked.

"We'll tackle that bridge when we come to it," replied Jack, "now go on," he urged.

"Come, let's head for where those two lava streams start to merge," Cordelia pointed ahead.

Saying our goodbyes for now, we made our way towards the lava streams, which quickly began to drop, with a path going between them. The path wound down until soon we were on the same level as the lava lake, which was a few hundred yards behind us now.

Ahead the lava streams ran into either side of a cavern, outside of which sat a raggedy old man.

"Err ... hello," I said, as I approached.

"Hey, what, who goes there!" said the old man looking straight at us with milky white eyes.

It was apparent the old man was blind. "Travellers," I replied, "looking for the Cauldron of Life."

"Well then, you have come to the right place," cackled the old man. "I am the keeper and seer; the guardian of the Cauldron of Life. It is a long time since I have had visitors here. Why do you seek the cauldron?"

"We have come to repair the fractured skull," I stated.

"The fractured skull; you have the fractured skull? Can it be true?"

"Yes, we have it."

"Get it out and pass it here; I must examine it and make sure it is the true fractured skull."

Carefully I removed the skull from my backpack and passed it to the old man. The old man received it reverently; there was always a deep respect and awe held by anyone who came into contact with the skull.

The old man ran his hands all over the skull and said excitedly, "Yes, yes, this is the skull! I can feel the power and the damage done. The true skull, it is hard to believe, after all these eons waiting here in the bowels of the earth. Finally the skull has returned, now to be repaired."

"But how do we repair it?" I asked.

"Patience young man, we must offer it to the cauldron, only the Cauldron of Life can heal the damage done."

"Can we see the Cauldron of Life?" I asked.

"Only those who can't see can truly see the cauldron; only the blind can see," said the old man, speaking in riddles.

"Is the cauldron in the chamber beyond?" Cordelia asked.

"Why yes, but if you want to see it you will have to wear these eye masks. The cauldron is not for mortal eyes; I should know."

He handed us each a black eye mask and told us to put them on tightly.

With some reticence we donned the eye masks. All at once my world became black and I could feel how it must be to be blind. Lacking sight, however, meant all my other senses became sharper. I could smell different odours amongst the overpowering smell of sulphur. I could smell the sweat on our bodies and the hint of a fragrance that Cordelia was wearing. My hearing became more acute too; I could hear the rushing lava streams to either side of me and the whirling roar ahead as they met. I knew without seeing that where the lava streams met there was a whirlpool of fire and lava.

"What about Trinity?" I asked, unsure of whether Trinity would be allowed in with us and, if so, if she would have to wear a mask too. I couldn't see Trinity agreeing to a mask.

"Trinity is your dog, yes? She is a strong dog and copes with her three legs well."

I wondered how the blind man knew that Trinity had three legs; his senses must be really acute!

"It would not be safe for her to enter the chamber of the cauldron," he continued. "She must remain outside and guard the entrance for us."

With that the old man whispered something into Trinity's ear, after which Trinity went over and assumed her guard position outside the chamber of the cauldron. There is more to this old man than meets the eye, I thought, bemused at how I struggle to get Trinity to obey even the most basic command and yet there she was guarding the chamber for the old man.

"Now, let us join our hands and I will lead you into the cavern," the old man stated. "Joshua, you hold the fractured skull," he instructed, handing me back the skull.

We linked hands and slowly the old man led us into the cavern. The heat was intense and sweat poured off us. "Don't mind the heat," advised the old man, "keep going." We did and soon the roar of the lava was deafening.

"We are in the chamber of the cauldron," shouted the old man. "Before us hangs the cauldron, filled with the waters of life, above a whirling pool of lava. Open your mind and your third eye will let you see the cauldron, empty your mind of all other thoughts other than the cauldron."

I tried to empty my mind but it was soon taken over by thoughts of home and my wife, who must by now be frantic with worry with Trinity and I missing for so long. Questions also went through my mind about whether this was real or not, or just part of my psychosis. I was still, after having been in this world for such a long time, struggling to believe in its reality. Slowly, however, I managed to calm these thoughts down and tuned into the roar of the lava. I focused on the lava meeting in a swirling pool below me and then tried to imagine a cauldron above it. Gradually a window opened up in my forehead and through this window I could see a bubbling cauldron of bright white light.

"I see it," I said, awestruck.

"Now take the skull and drop it into the cauldron," said the old man.

I did as he said and as I dropped the skull into the cauldron, it was immediately immersed in swirling white light. The light was then sucked in through the eye sockets and ejected out through the mouth, then back into the eye sockets again in a continuous cycle. Some of the light then began to leak through the fracture, until more and more light passed through the fracture. As it exited the fracture, the light turned golden in colour and soon the whole skull was surrounded by a golden halo. Then I watched through my third eye as the fracture gradually began to close, millimetre by millimetre, until eventually in a blinding flash of rainbow hued light the skull closed up altogether and the fracture was healed. Before me now, in a swirling pool of light, spun a transparent golden skull, glowing from within. It had come alive in the cauldron of life; the fractured skull was no longer the fractured skull, it was whole!

"Now take the skull, for it will speak only to the healer," said the old man.

Slowly I reached in to the swirling pool of light and felt blissful energy flow up through me, filling my body with euphoria. I grasped the skull, which vibrated with my touch, and then golden light passed through me mixing with the white light, and my mind was filled with the knowledge of ages. Slowly I was taken back in time, witnessing everything the skull had seen and realised it had been around for eons.

I was shown images of my own world where mankind tried to harness the energy of the skull for its own greed and ended up fracturing it, thus causing disruption to the realm of the twilight moon. I saw an image of the moon splitting into three moons: one moon sank beneath the ocean with the City of Shells, the second moon spun into space to orbit another planet and the final moon stayed in the realm of the twilight moon, weak and diminished.

The skull then spoke to me, its words running through me and appearing inside my head, "You must heal the twilight moon; the twilight moon must be made three, for three is the order of the realm. I have the power to heal the moon but first you must find my twin skull, the midnight skull."

With these words I felt the power dim inside the skull and it spoke no more. From outside the chamber, Trinity started barking and I remembered she was on guard duty.

"Quick, we must leave the chamber and take the skull to safety. There are other forces who desire the skull for their own needs and we must not let it fall into the wrong hands.

Chapter 17 – Flight with the Skull

On leaving the chamber, we found Trinity there barking. Quickly we removed the blindfolds to see what she was barking at, but could see nothing.

"I'm not sure what Trinity is barking at, but she must be able to sense something that we can't," I said.

"It is the Shadow Dancer," replied the old man, "he is seldom seen and is nothing more than a shadow himself. Although he hides in the shadows, his reach is far and he is very powerful. He can manipulate shadows to for his own evil purposes. From now on a shadow may not always be what you expect it to be; keep an eye on the shadows. He seeks the skull and will stop at nothing to get it. You must flee, it is your only hope. He is very dangerous and cannot be allowed to get the skull."

"But where do we run to?" I asked.

"There is more than one way to cross The Devil's Forge. Come, I will show you."

We came to the edge of The Devil's Forge, but I could still see no way across.

"But how can we cross that lava with no bridge over it?" I queried.

"Who said anything about going over it," replied the old man, who started rolling a large rock to one side, "I was planning on you going under it. This tunnel leads right under The Devil's Forge and climbs to the plateau on the other side. Now, hurry, you must be quick. I will roll the rock back after you; remember the Shadow Dancer is tracking you and the skull; keep an eye on the shadows and listen for Trinity barking for she can sense him."

We thanked him and quickly climbed down inside the tunnel, which the old man sealed off behind us. Thankfully the tunnel gave off a natural red glow, so we could see to move along it. We could feel the heat of The Devil's Forge above us, but the tunnel was safe and kept the lava out. Soon we began to climb and I hoped the tunnel would not be sealed off when we got to the other end. My fears were unfounded as we emerged beneath a bush on the plateau overlooking The Devil's Forge.

Quickly I found the passage that led back to the others and crawled through it.

"How did you get here?" asked Captain Jack.

"I walked on fire," I joked, "or should I say, I walked underneath fire."

"You can be very cryptic at times," moaned Captain Jack.

"We came back underneath The Devil's Forge through a tunnel," I explained.

"Now you make sense," replied Captain Jack.

We soon crawled back through the passage to join the others and the party of the skull was reunited. I explained to Jack, Billy and Splinter about the Shadow Dancer, and how he was after the skull. I also told them about the midnight skull and how we needed to find it.

"So we've made it to The Devil's Forge, found the Cauldron of Life, healed the fractured skull, and now we have to find the midnight skull; anyone got any ideas?" I asked.

"I think I read something about the midnight skull in the Codex Historicus," said Cordelia. "It relates to another realm connected to the Twilight Realm known as the Midnight Realm. It says, 'The third twilight moon passed from the Twilight Realm to the midnight realm. It is here that the midnight skull can be found, the sister skull to the twilight skull, sometimes known as the fractured skull. The midnight realm can be found on the dark side of the Twilight Realm.'"

"But the dark side is just a myth," replied Captain Jack, "a place beyond the great ocean where darkness and ghouls are found. A place that scares children with bedtime stories."

"Perhaps it's not a myth," suggested Cordelia, "Perhaps there is such a place beyond the great ocean?"

"Then we must find a ship big and fast enough to sail there," said Captain Jack. "I'll captain her, if you are willing to join me on such a voyage of exploration?"

"Yes," we all agreed. "So where are we to find such a ship I asked?"

"That's easy," said Captain Jack, "we need to go to the largest port on the great ocean, Oceania ... only there will we find a vessel worthy of such a voyage."

"We better get moving quickly, before the Shadow Dancer finds us," I stated.

"Who or what is the Shadow Dancer?" asked Jack, Billy and Splinter.

"The Shadow Dancer is a shadow fiend who is after the skull to use for his own evil purposes. He can manipulate shadows and cause great harm. The guardian of the cauldron warned us to flee for he is very dangerous. Keep watching the shadows for any sign of him," I explained.

"I'm not scared of any shadows," said Captain Jack, but his face belied his true fears as his eyes scoured the shadows for any sign of the Shadow Dancer.

"Come on, let's go," I said, as I glanced into the shadows and saw a flicker of movement that shouldn't be there out of the corner of my eye.

Why did it have to be shadows I thought? Shadows have often haunted me as a symptom of my psychosis. I have frequently seen shadows when they shouldn't be there. Once, while driving home alone in the dark, I remember seeing a shadow cast across the road in front of me, its dark brooding presence resembling that of the Grim Reaper. Now I was in a world that I didn't know was real or not with shadows haunting me once again, only this time they were surely out to get me as the keeper of the skull. The difference between the real and unreal was becoming a blur and I was not sure if my mind could cope.

We made the long journey, past streams of lava, back up to the surface. On many an instance one or more of us spotted something in the shadows, only for it to disappear again. Whatever it was the shadow dancer wasn't going to manifest yet, but I couldn't help thinking it was biding its time.

We finally made it back to the surface, this time popping our heads from out of a manhole cover in the pollution filled streets of Old Smoky. The tower blocks loomed up above us, dark and brooding, grey with grit and grime.

We made our way back towards the railway station, constantly aware of the deep shadows cast by the skyscrapers under the blue moonlight.

Suddenly Trinity started barking and then Cordelia screamed. Quickly I turned to see Cordelia struggling in the grasp of a man - wait, no, not the man, but the man's shadow! I had never seen anything like it! Quickly I grasped Cordelia's hand and dragged her out of the shadow's grasp.

Run," I shouted to the others and we all started running, with Billy leading the way.

Every person that we passed their shadows reached out towards us; how were we going to get away and escape the clutches of the Shadow Dancer? He was everywhere and it was hard to avoid people and their shadows. We took to running down the middle of the street, dodging in and out of traffic. The traffic was all huge steam powered contraptions, vehicles of all shapes and sizes churning out steam and smoke into the sky. Several times one of us nearly got run over, but still we kept going.

Finally we reached the station and Billy ushered us on-board an express train that was about to depart. We climbed on-board and selected a cabin to ourselves just as the train departed. We waved Billy goodbye, thanking him for his help, and we were on our way. The gargantuan black steel train soon picked up speed and Trinity settled down. We had left the Shadow Dancer in the city, but how long until he picked up our trail again I wondered?

As we sat on the train to Oceania I felt my mood dip. Sensing this, as she always does, Trinity put her head on my lap giving me the comfort I so needed. I couldn't help thinking about my beautiful wife waiting at home, frantic, not knowing where I was. How could she know that I was in another world and whether of my own making I knew not? The twilight world passed by in a blur, which was both due to the speed of the train and my state of mind. My eyes stopped focusing on things, letting everything blur into one in this monochrome world I now inhabited.

Captain Jack brought me out of my trance. "What's up mate?" he asked with concern in his tone and gently put a hand on my shoulder.

"I don't know, I just feel lost in a world that's not mine."

"Don't worry, we're here with you and will make sure you make it back to your own home. You're a genuine guy and I am sure your world is missing you loads."

"Why thank you Jack, you are the friends I need right now."

"We're all here for you," said Splinter.

"Yes, me too," added Cordelia.

Slowly I started to come out of my dip. I looked out of the window and saw fantastical trees, taller than skyscrapers; massive multicoloured birds with their wings shimmering iridescent in the blue moonlight and thought to myself that maybe this world wasn't so bad after all; but still I missed my wife.

The port of Oceania was massive when we came to it, stretching for miles across a large bay. The ocean itself was a lovely deep blue, heightened by the blue twilight sky. All the buildings were either pale blue or white and reminded me of a Greek fishing port, but on a massive scale. The port itself harboured some huge sailing ships, bigger than any I have ever seen in my own world.

"This," announced Jack as we approached, "is Oceania, the biggest port in the Twilight Realm. If you have a soul for the sea this is the place to be!"

Chapter 18 – Oceania

The port was bustling with men pushing barrels, women mending nets and fishing boats unloading their glistening cargo of fish; the scent of which pervaded the air of the port.

"We must find the Mermaid Inn," said Captain Jack, "It is there we will find out about the best ships in the harbour for such a voyage. It will just be the small matter of persuading the captain of the ship to take us on this high seas adventure."

"Sounds like a plan," I replied. "Good luck with persuading the captain though."

"Ahoy there," shouted Jack to a sailor just passing bye, "can you tell us where we can find the Mermaid Inn?"

"The Mermaid you be wanting," he replied. "Well that's easy, just follow the sailors getting off that ship that's just docked, that's where they'll be heading."

"Why thank you, I should have guessed that myself."

We quickly made our way down to the docks and followed the group of travel weary sailors as they made their way to their favourite watering hole. The Mermaid Inn turned out to be a rickety, slanting, white clapperboard faced old inn, with a statue of a well endowed mermaid at the front; it looked every bit the sailors' inn.

Inside was smoky, with sailors singing sea shanties and buxom barmaids serving beer frothing over pewter tankards.

"What will it be?" asked Jack. As ever, the first to find his way to the bar.

"Mine's a rum," I replied, keeping with the nautical spirit of the place.

"Just water for me," replied Splinter, "Alcohol plays havoc with my crystals."

"Make mine a white wine," answered Cordelia, surprising us in choosing an alcoholic drink.

Meanwhile, Trinity found a water bowl by the door and was busy lapping at that.

Captain Jack ordered the drinks, including a large rum for himself and asked if the barmaid wanted anything.

"Don't mind if I do," answered the barmaid, "make mine a white wine like the lady here."

Captain Jack winked at her and asked, "Do you know which the fastest boat in the harbour is at the moment?"

"You listen to the sailors and their boat is always the fastest boat. If you really want the fastest boat, better ask old Red Beard over there; no one knows boats better than he does."

"Thanks," said Jack, "What does he drink?"

"Rum of course."

"I'd better have a rum then please, if I want to loosen Red Beard's tongue."

"Good idea, here you go," said the barmaid with a smile.

We went over to Red Beard, who was deep in conversation with his parrot.

"Sorry to interrupt," said Jack.

"Hey ... err, no problem, can't get a damn word out of this parrot other than 'A bottle of rum'."

"If it's a bottle of rum you be wanting, then will this do?" Captain Jack asked, handing him the rum.

"Why, that's mighty kind of you stranger."

"Captain Jack's, the name," said Jack extending his hand.

"Red Beard's mine," said the sailor taking Jack's hand and gripping it in a vice-like grip.

With some relief Red Beard let go and Jack could feel the blood flow back into his hand again. "Do you know which is the fastest ship in port?" asked Jack, getting straight to the point.

"A fast ship you be wanting, what can that be for I wonder?"

Jack could see he was not going to get any information out of Red Beard without disclosing some information himself. He leant over and whispered to Red Beard, "We're planning a voyage to discover the dark side and the legendary treasure that's to be found there."

"It's a good job you are whispering this to me; these sailors are a superstitious lot and they've heard bad tales about the dark side. Not that it's true of course. That said, what's this you're saying about legendary treasure?" said Red Beard with a glint in his eye.

Jack knew he had him hooked; Red Beard looked just the type of treasure seeking sailor that would venture somewhere like the dark side if there was treasure involved.

"Well apparently there is a city of gold just waiting to be found; that is, if there is a sailor brave enough and a ship fast enough?"

"Well, I might just know of a ship," said Red Beard, "but if we are to persuade the captain you will need me on-board."

"You look just like the type of sea shark we need with us," said Captain Jack, spitting on his hand and offering it to Red Beard.

Red beard spat on his hand and they clasped hands, reminding Jack not to do this too often as the blood went out of his hand once again.

"Right you are matey, now for the ship. They say this ship glides through the water like a ghost and is faster than the wind."

"Is she faster than the shadows though?" asked Captain Jack.

"What a strange question, but I think even shadows will struggle to keep up with her under full sail."

"Then this sounds like the ship for me. What's her name?"

"She's called Stormchaser and her captain is none other than Deadeye Jim, the cruellest, most wicked captain ever to sail the great ocean."

"Sounds like a nice chap," I said.

"Don't go messing with him sonny, unless you want to end up as fish bait!" warned Red Beard.

"So how do we get this dirty, greedy, low down, ruthless captain to sail with us to the dark side?" asked Captain Jack?

"You offer him riches beyond his wildest dreams, just like you did me; greed always wins out with his sort."

"Right, when can we meet him?" Captain Jack asked.

"We can go over to his ship right now if you like?"

"Let's do it, no time like the present."

We left the Inn, thankfully before Jack had managed to have too many rums and headed back to the port.

"There she is." Red Beard pointed to a tall ship moored just near the entrance to the harbour. The ship was long and sleek and all black. Her masts pierced the sky they were so tall.

"She's a mighty fine ship," said Captain Jack, "let's hope Deadeye agrees to this mission."

When we arrived at the ship it was even bigger than we had anticipated when viewing it from a distance. It was huge - at least twice as long as any other ship in the harbour.

"Ahoy there Deadeye," called Red Beard, "permission to come on board."

A tall figure emerged from the captain's quarters, wearing a long black cape, with his hair tied back and a patch over his eye. "If it isn't Old Red Beard. Now I wonder what you'll be wanting; some darn fool mission I expect. Better come on board."

We crossed the gangplank onto the ship and were met by Deadeye himself. "So come on Red Beard, what is it you are wanting? I know for sure you didn't come to say hello."

"Well it's like this you see ... I was talking to Captain Jack here and he mentioned treasure, like you've never seen before; a city of gold. The only trouble is it ... err ... can be found on the dark side."

"The dark side, surely you don't believe in that!" retorted Deadeye.

"It's up to you," said Jack, "but there is such a city and there is such a thing as the dark side and I believe your fine ship is the only one capable of getting us there. So, how about it?"

"Why should I believe you?"

"Because I have the fractured skull, which is fractured no more. Show him the golden skull Joshua."

I took out the skull and showed old Deadeye it.

"Well I never! I thought that it was just a myth. If you have the fractured skull, then maybe there just might be something such as the dark side and if anyone is going to find this city of gold, then it's me. Count me in, we sail tomorrow."

Chapter 19 – Journey to the Dark Side

It was a fair wind when we set sail and the black ship glided out of the harbour. As soon as we left the harbour we set full sail for the north. The speed of the boat was invigorating as the crew worked as one, climbing the masts and trimming the sails.

I spotted a sailor with one arm and a peg leg and asked Deadeye, who was at the helm, "How did he lose his limbs, was it a terrible sea battle?"

"What, old peg leg, no, fastest man aloft was peg leg."

"Then how did he come to have only one arm and one leg then?"

"Oh, he was also the fastest man below," chuckled Deadeye.

I could see that Deadeye didn't have too much concern for his crew and decided to make sure I wasn't considered surplus to requirements.

"When we get to the dark side I will make sure we find the lost city of gold."

"That's why you're aboard matey and not seven fathoms down."

I wondered if he had a good side and thought, probably not.

I went and stood at the prow, wind blowing through my hair, and I felt like I was flying; it truly was a sensational boat. I could taste the salt in the sea breeze in my mouth and thought that yes, life was good at sea. It wasn't long, however, before I changed my mind. The steady breeze started to gust and a shout from the crow's nest came: "Storm clouds ahead Captain."

"All hands to deck," shouted Deadeye, "Get those sails down and secure everything."

He looked at me and the others, "Joshua, you had better get your party inside, I don't want to lose those who are going to find me my treasure."

So much for worrying about us; still we weren't expendable, so long as he believed we were the key to finding this mythical city of gold. We followed his command and made our way into the Captain's cabin. By now the sea was getting rough and the ship was starting to roll from side to side; my stomach was also starting to roll and I felt like I might have to empty its contents at any moment. To try and ward off the sea sickness I looked out of the cabin's leaded windows and saw the black clouds coming, like an ink black blanket in the sky. Soon the blackness was on us with the wind howling through the masts and rigging. I felt sure one of the masts would snap sooner or later.

A blinding flash filled the sky and I saw a man struck by lightning on the mast, then tumble into the watery grave of the ocean. A massive clap of thunder followed and there were yells from the sailors on deck. Soon we were in the heart of the thunderstorm and the sea and sky became a whirling maelstrom around us. Such was the power of the wind that I saw a sailor whipped off the deck and flung through the air past our cabin window into the depths of the freezing ocean beyond.

Waves came up to meet the windows as the boat rolled from side to side ever more violently. It could surely only be a matter of time before the boat turned right over and sank, I thought. Water must also be washing into the bowels of the ship which would make us sink. As the ship rocked we were flung around the cabin like rag dolls. Quickly I braced myself in a corner and managed to keep from being bashed around anymore.

The storm raged for hours, by the end of which there was nothing left in my stomach to bring up; I had completely emptied it. By some miracle we survived the storm, but was the ship intact?

Deadeye came into the cabin, his black cloak ripped and shredded by the storm, his hair wild about his shoulders. "That's the blackest storm I have ever been through; still Stormchaser made it through as she always does. However, the main mast is snapped in two. We are going to have to splint it. How are my party of adventurers? Intact I hope? We still have that treasure to find."

I looked around at the rest of our group; they all looked shaken but I couldn't see any visible injuries. "Aye, we all made it through," said Captain Jack.

"Good, I'm off to find the ship's carpenter then; he better not have been swept overboard, at least not until the mast is mended that is."

"Nice man," I said to the rest of our group after he had left.

"As I said, he is the meanest, dirtiest, nastiest, most evil captain in the whole of the great ocean," said Red Beard.

"I'll try and not get on the wrong side of him," I replied.

"He doesn't have a good side," responded Red Beard.

Needing some fresh air, after the turbulence of the storm, I ventured outside. The ship's carpenter was already at work repairing the main mast. God help him if he can't fix it, I thought.

Deadeye was rushing around the deck, shouting orders and endeavouring to get Stormchaser shipshape again. By the frantic way his crew responded to his commands, that wouldn't be long I thought.

Soon, with the help of deck hands, the carpenter had the mast back in place and firmly splinted, while the rest of the deck had been cleared of debris and vital equipment put back.

Order restored, Deadeye didn't waste any time in getting going again.

"Hoist the sails," he commanded, and we were soon skimming along the ocean water again.

Taking the ship's wheel, Deadeye set course due north, destination the dark side if it existed. I couldn't help thinking I had already been to the dark side when we went through that storm. The dark side couldn't be worse than that could it?

I questioned once more the reality of the world I was currently experiencing and wondered if the dark side was a manifestation of my own dark psyche. Also was this mysterious Shadow Dancer who was pursuing us yet another manifestation of my own mind? I questioned it all, yet it all seemed so real; how was I to tell what was real and what was not?

I wondered where Trinity was as I suddenly realised that I hadn't seen her since the storm set in. I went back to the cabin and looked around for her. I eventually found her fast asleep under the captain's table; the storm hadn't affected her at all and she had slept through it all. Trinity certainly had better sea legs than I.

I left Trinity to her dreams and went back outside again. The storm clouds were clearing and moonlight pierced through their dark umber umbrella, sending a shaft of light down on the ship like a spotlight. Long shadows spread out along the deck and I immediately began thinking of the Shadow Dancer, hoping he wasn't there amongst them.

I started pacing up and down the deck, trying to avoid stepping into shadows. It is amazing how hard it is to avoid shadows; not something I had thought of before or tried to do for that matter. As I made my way back and forth along the deck, I couldn't help thinking there was something sinister hiding in the shadows and on more than one occasion I could have sworn I saw a shadow move unexpectedly out of the corner of my eye. Something told me the Shadow Dancer was here and was just waiting for the right moment to strike.

A cloud moved across the moon again, swallowing up the shadows with it. I felt the tension ease, like a sigh or a breath of wind blowing away. Hastily I made my way back to the cabin, and the others, before the moon cast its light again.

When I was back safely in the cabin I told the others about my experiences and fears of the shadows.

"I believe the Shadow Dancer has followed us here and is now onboard biding his time."

"Oh no, not the Shadow Dancer," said Cordelia, shivering at the thought. "I was hoping we had left him behind."

"Don't worry Cordelia," said Captain Jack, "We won't let the Shadow Dancer touch you."

"Let's keep an eye out for each other and keep a lookout for unusual shadows," said Splinter.

"Good idea," I agreed.

"Now let's go out and help the crew with the tidying up, Deadeye may not have a good side, but I sure as hell don't want to make him think we are surplus to requirements," stated Jack.

We got to work clearing the decks, all the time keeping an eye on the shadows in the background. The clouds soon cleared altogether and we felt under constant threat from the long shadows the moon was casting on deck; yet still the Shadow Dancer didn't strike, but I was sure that he was here with us.

I had an idea that didn't make me feel too comfortable and decided to mention it to the others.

"I think the shadow dancer is here, but he is waiting for something. I think he knows about the other skull and is waiting for us to find the skull before he strikes."

"I think you are right," said Splinter, "The power of the two skulls together must be phenomenal."

"There is one thing, however, if the dark side really is dark then there won't be many shadows in which he can hide," I stated.

"Good point," replied Jack thoughtfully.

The journey across the great ocean became a test of endurance. The sea went on forever with the sky and the ocean meeting in a twilight blue kiss, merging as if one. It felt as though we were in a great void, sailing into space and that we would never see land again. At least, during the storm, there were waves and clouds; now everything had become a featureless blur. With there being no day or night in the Twilight Realm, I had no idea how many days had passed on the voyage, but it went on for what seemed like an eternity. It felt like we were in some kind of purgatory awaiting judgement; a judgement that I didn't relish because, from all I had heard about the dark side, it didn't sound like a pleasant place.

A darkness on the horizon was the first sign that the end of our journey was in sight and that the dark side was more than a fairytale told to children.

The darkness loomed bigger and bigger, like black ink spreading across a blue canvas. Soon it became so dark that we had to light all the lanterns on the ship to be able to see at all. Then the darkness engulfed us and for the first time since my arrival in the Twilight Realm, I experienced something that was not twilight but, despite its darkness, wasn't night either, for there was no moon or stars, just blackness. It was as if we had been swallowed by a black hole in which no light could escape. It was a frightening and lonely place; a place for lost souls and spirits, not for the living.

Chapter 20 – The Dark Side

The darkness matched the darkness inside me, a deep black pit into which I was falling. I missed my wife, my world, my home; would I ever find a way back, I wondered? Trinity, detecting my dark mood, came over to me and nuzzled her head against me. She is ever present to comfort me in my darkest hour; I don't know what I would do without her. She has a sixth sense when something is wrong and is always there for me, protecting and loyal.

Splinter came over to me and said, "I am uneasy in this darkness, it is not natural and doesn't feel right."

"It's as if time had stopped," I replied. "There are no dimensions in this world; time and direction have no place here. It is just an empty void ... except I know it isn't; I can sense other things such as spirits that don't want us here. We are intruders, trespassers in a world we can't see."

"I know how you feel," agreed Splinter, "there is something out there, I just can't see it; something, someone, spirits or beings that are beyond our comprehension, malevolent and waiting for us."

Our conversation was interrupted by the arrival of Deadeye. We were in his cabin and lanterns were casting shadows upon the floor; another fear I'd rather not think about.

"Right then, you were right about the dark side existing, so now where's my city of gold?"

"I'd say keep heading north and we'll find it," I replied, hoping that this would satisfy him.

"North, hey? Have you looked at the compass recently?" Jack handed me the ship's compass.

I looked at it and was shocked to see the needle spinning round.

"I believe we have entered another dimension here without direction or time. We must find another way to navigate."

"That's why I brought you along and why you are not six fathoms under with a rock tied to your ankles," replied Deadeye.

"Seeing as you put it like that, perhaps there is a way to navigate. Give me time to think about it and I will come up with a way."

"I'll give you an hour and if you don't come up with something by the time I get back you're fish bait," said Deadeye, leaving the cabin.

"What are we going to do?" I asked the others.

"I'm not sure, but we had better come up with something quick," replied Jack.

"Let's take a lantern, go up to the prow and see what we can see, or can't as the case may be."

"Good idea, come on then," answered Jack, taking a lantern and leading the way.

As we walked up to the prow I could hear whispering voices in the air. This immediately alarmed me, for one of the symptoms of my psychosis is hearing voices; if it wasn't my psychosis, however, it was just as frightening, as these disembodied voices could be spirits or ghosts.

I couldn't make out what the voices were whispering; it was either in a different language or too indistinct. Whatever they were saying, though, sent a chill down my spine.

When we arrived at the prow I asked the others, "Did you hear whispering voices as we crossed the deck?"

"No," came the communal reply, with Cordelia adding, "I could sense something else there and felt something cold touch my cheek though."

"Yes," agreed Jack, "There is definitely something out there, but it's not showing itself, whatever kind of being it is."

Their answers only compounded my fears; one that I was hearing voices as part of my psychosis and two that there was something out there and that it didn't feel too friendly. How were we to navigate though? For some reason I felt a compulsion to take the crystal skull out of my backpack. Its smoky quartz shimmered in the lamplight, then the most extraordinary thing happened. The inside of the skull began to light up on its own; flickers of blue zipped across the skull, like the firing of synapses in the brain, in an electric dance. Then the blue coalesced in the eye sockets getting brighter and brighter until two bright blue beams shone out from the skull pointing to the left of the prow.

"I think we have our navigation system," I said, "the skull must be detecting its sister skull and pointing the way."

"Crikey, that's quite something," replied Splinter, "I wish my crystals could do that."

Spotting the blue beams of light shining out from the prow, Deadeye came up to us to find out what was going on. I explained:

"The skull is showing us the way; we need to follow the beams coming from its eyes."

"I knew the promise of a watery grave would focus your minds; I'll get my men to mount it on the prow and plot a course by the beams of light. It had better lead us to this city of gold though."

"It will lead us there," I replied, knowing full well it was leading us to the other skull. Still, we would tackle that bridge when we got to it.

With the skull mounted on the prow we were soon sailing in a direct line with the blue beams of light, which could pierce the darkness in a way no ordinary light could. Even the wind seemed to be in our favour, blowing behind us so that we didn't have to tack.

The journey seemed to go on forever; the darkness swamped us, apart from where the blue beams of light penetrated it. The whispering voices plagued me even though I couldn't understand them; they were insidious and felt full of loathing. I became more and more convinced that they were a conjuring of my mind, especially as no one else heard them. Often I would see shadows move in unexpected ways and I knew that the Shadow Dancer was here with us, just biding his time; if he too wasn't a figment of my imagination projected from my mind. I was becoming more and more unstable, unsure of my sanity and where I was. This world, or should I say these worlds, could not be real. Surely there must be some deep psychological explanation for it all, I thought without conviction, because everything felt real; if anything more real than my own world.

The journey wasn't without incident for a fear plagued the whole ship and the crew of Stormchaser began to wear talismans and curse the sea. Their fears weren't unfounded, for one sailor was found screaming and fighting with an unseen assailant before leaping into the sea and drowning. He wasn't the only one either. A total of three other sailors went the same way and died a watery fate.

Eventually we saw a light appear ahead of us, glowing a warm yellow in the blackness beyond.

"That's the City of Gold," exclaimed Deadeye, "it really exists!" Taking the spyglass he looked out to see if his hopes were true, but could see nothing more than the golden glow.

As we got closer, to my amazement and relief, features began to appear in the golden light and glittering before us was an island with a citadel made out of gold.

Chapter 21 – Citadel of Gold

"There's your City of Gold Deadeye," said Captain Jack, "a shiny citadel made from gold."

"Why it sure is gold, the colour of my dreams," said Deadeye, "enough for all of us I think. You really have found us the City of Gold. Full sail ahead, gold awaits us me hearties!"

As we approached I was expecting to be met by a greeting party or, worse still, a cannon fire. Everywhere was spookily quiet though, which in its way was more unnerving than being under attack. Something sinister pervaded the air, something that waited in the silence. Even the whisperings I had been hearing had gone. It was if those very spirits that had haunted us on the journey were scared to go there. I didn't like the feeling and my gut instinct was to keep away. I didn't have a choice, however, not with Deadeye's eye for gold; there was only one place we were going and I felt like a fly going into a spider's web. To make matters worse I could feel the presence of the Shadow Dancer, with shadows becoming more active in ways they were not supposed to. I didn't know what to fear most, the Shadow Dancer or whatever awaited us on this golden island.

The boat pulled up in a deserted harbour; the harbour itself was not gold but the citadel above it was. Something warned me not to go into the citadel. Whatever that feeling was it definitely didn't affect Deadeye and his men, for as soon as they had disembarked they made their way to the Citadel of Gold.

I voiced my concerns to the rest of the party:

"I don't think we should enter the citadel. There's something not quite right about it that makes me uneasy."

"I agree," replied Cordelia, "all that glitters is not gold. There is something more than gold in that citadel and it is definitely evil; I can feel it."

"So where shall we go?" asked Jack.

"I am not sure," I replied, "but we need to find the midnight skull. Let's take the skull from its place at the prow and see if it will lead us to the skull."

"Good idea," agreed Splinter, lifting the skull from the prow and handing it to me, "you lead the way."

Taking the skull, and with Trinity beside me, I set off with the beams of blue light still leading the way into the island. To my great relief and everyone else's, once we got to the harbours edge the beams of light directed us away from the golden citadel and onto a path that led around it. By this time the treasure hungry crew of Stormchaser had all entered the citadel, but strangely we could hear nothing of them. The silence was scarier than any scream or cry for help could be; it had a ring of finality to it and I wondered what could have happened to the crew.

"Do you hear that?" I asked the others.

"No," came the communal reply.

"Precisely, don't you think a crew of treasure hungry sailors would be making a huge noise in a fabled citadel of gold?"

"There's something not quite right," agreed Jack, "there is no way I am going into that citadel, gold or no gold."

"Let's keep following this path around it," I suggested. "The skull is taking us that way anyway."

"Keep an eye on the shadows," stated Cordelia, "I am sure the Shadow Dancer is here with us."

"Yes," I agreed, "The glow off the golden citadel is casting a lot of shadows and they don't seem to be behaving the way normal shadows do."

"I think we will be alright until we find the midnight skull," said Splinter, "and when we do, that's when the Shadow Dancer will strike."

"Let's keep an eye out all the same; he might decide to pick us off one by one," I stated.

"Uggg, I hope not," replied Cordelia, "I can still feel his cold shadowy hands on me, like steel cobwebs, insubstantial but strong."

"Try not to think about it Cordelia, we'll all keep a lookout for you."

"Thank you." Cordelia smiled in an uneasy way.

The skull kept leading us around the Golden Citadel, which was vaster than I expected it to be, going on for miles, all the time casting golden light down upon us.

I kept looking into the shadows that moved in peculiar ways, always just out of shape from the object or person from which the shadow was cast. I kept feeling the reaching shadowy fingers at the back of my neck, but when I turned round they weren't there. I tried to walk around the shadows cast by trees and rocks, but it became impossible. It was as if their shadows contained liquid shadows within and I felt as though I were walking through a thin soup that was engulfing me. I knew the Shadow Dancer wasn't far away and that he was just biding his time, yet making his presence known by casting these liquid shadows within shadows.

"Can anyone else feel the shadows?" I asked tentatively.

"Yes," replied everyone, "I can feel something cold and clammy every time I step into one," added Cordelia.

Trinity was even more sensitive to the shadows, turning round and barking at her own shadow on a number of occasions as if it belonged to another dog.

As we made our way around the golden citadel a mountain came into view, looming dark against the golden glow of the citadel. Even though it had a brooding presence it at once felt better than the citadel, from which we had still heard no sounds emanate. The mountain was different, however, as a low hum could be heard, and as we finally rounded the citadel the blue beams of the eyes pointed straight at it.

Guided by the skull we soon found ourselves on a track going up the mountain. Despite getting higher and higher, the temperature remained constant and there was no snow on the mountain. As we neared the summit we noticed the peak resembled a skull hewn out of black rock. When we finally approached the skull we noticed that the pathway entered the mountain through the jaws of the skull, which were illuminated by a yellow glow coming from inside.

"Do you think we should enter?" asked Cordelia.

"We've come all this way, I don't think we should turn back now," answered Captain Jack.

"I agree," said Splinter.

"Ok, the skull cave it is then," I accepted. "I'll go first," I volunteered, leading the way.

I stepped through the jaws of the skull and into the light inside with the others following close behind. Then several things happened at once. Trinity started barking like mad and shadows cast by the interior light started reaching out towards us. Cordelia screamed as she was grasped by one of the shadows. Quickly I pulled her away but as I did another shadow started reaching for me and I could see no escape. The last thing I remember seeing, as the shadow engulfed me, was a crystal skull on a plinth in the centre of the cave, glowing a deep midnight blue. Then there was blackness and I could feel myself being squeezed in the folds of a shadowy cloak.

Chapter 22 – The Midnight Skull

 A midnight blue light pierced the blackness that engulfed me; its light had an intensity and depth that I had never known before. Rather than shining on me, it penetrated through me in a way that it would through glass, except I was not made of glass like splinter. This was a light that didn't get blocked by objects and, because of this, didn't cast any shadows. The shadows dispersed around us so that all that was left was an all-consuming blue light radiating out from the midnight skull.
The light filled me with a strange energy; I could feel millions of stars and moons shooting through me, filling me with light and memories of the cosmos. What was this mysterious blue light, cast in a midnight hue, effervescent with stars and moonlight? It was as if the universe was captured within the skull and was radiating out through me. I felt alive with new memories, as if I had awoken for the first time, born into a new world. Yet had I awoken, or was I asleep in my own imaginary world? Was all this a figment of my mind, a hallucination brought on by psychosis? It was hard to refute, yet harder still to accept. How far had I travelled from my own world. I longed for home, but the magic of the world I now inhabited, in my mind at least, touched me with its beauty. Whatever reality turned out to be, I knew the Twilight Realm and its associated worlds would now forever be a part of me.

"Do you feel the energy?" asked Cordelia.

"Yes, I can feel it coursing through me like a million fireflies lighting up inside me," replied Splinter.

"I feel alive in a way that I have never felt before," added Captain Jack.

"I feel the energy of a million suns rising inside me," I agreed.

"The dark side is an empty receptacle waiting to be filled. I believe the midnight skull encompasses all the dark side and is waiting to be released back into the dark realm. If we can find the key to releasing this power we can make the dark realm whole again," said Cordelia.

"The key I think lies within the Citadel of Gold. Whatever evil is present in the Citadel of Gold holds the key to releasing what is trapped in the midnight skull. Only this key can restore the dark realm and dispel the void that is the dark side," I answered.

"Then it is to the Citadel of Gold we must go," said Captain Jack, "but I am wary of what happened to the crew of the Stormchaser; for there has been a deafening silence since that rowdy crew of treasure seekers entered the citadel and that doesn't bode well I fear."

"Let us carry the midnight skull into the citadel, for I believe it will offer us some protection," stated Splinter.

"I think you are right," I agreed, "there is a power in the skull that I think is even greater than whatever evil lies within the Citadel of Gold. We have two skulls now and we must find a way of unleashing their power to make the twilight moon three and restore parity to the realm. I believe the answer lies within the Citadel of Gold."

"Let us make our way there then," said Jack, heading towards the exit of the cave.

"Yes, let us do so," agreed Cordelia following.

We all followed Jack and Cordelia out of the skull cave and back down the mountain towards the Citadel of Gold. The path was easy and the citadel beckoned us in its shimmering golden light. The midnight skull still cast its midnight light through us, safely dispelling any shadows on the way down. I hadn't realised there were so many different types of light until now; I always thought that light obeyed the Newtonian laws of physics, but the midnight blue light changed all this with its blue starlit glow fizzing through us.

It wasn't long until we came to the entrance to the citadel, golden and inviting. Even though all I wanted was to return to my own world, I couldn't help but be enticed by all the gold that made up the citadel. Everyone has a little bit of a treasure seeker hidden inside them, some more than most. It was this factor that I believed was at the heart of the citadel, a kind of sugar trap to entice people in, but what waited beyond those golden gates? I was not sure I wanted to know.

Holding the midnight skull before me, tentatively I led our party through the gates to the citadel. All remained silent, then the world changed as we stepped through. Before us stood a giant spider in a rocky cavern. Cocooned in spider silk and hanging from the ceiling were the crew of Stormchaser, waiting their turn to be eaten by the giant spider. The spider must have been a good six feet high with a leg span of at least fifteen feet. It was covered in black hair, its eyes glowed red and its fangs dripped a mixture of venom and blood.

Suddenly red laser-like beams projected from its eyes towards us, shattering on the blue glow emitting from the midnight skull around us. Then in response the midnight skull sent intense beams of blue light directly back at the spider, striking it in its twitching abdomen. The spider emitted an ear piercing shriek and writhed in pain. It sent beam after beam of red light from its glowing eyes, each beam harmlessly deflected off our blue shield, whilst the skull sent more blue rays back at the spider. The spider, seeing that the beams weren't working, came at us, its jaws wide open. Just as it was upon us, a mighty blue bolt shot out from the skull and stopped it dead in its tracks. It rolled over and screamed the most hideous cry I have ever heard, kicking its eight legs in the air; then all of a sudden it was still, dead in its lair, no longer a threat to man.

I looked at the others, who had horror in their eyes. "Now we know the grisly fate of the sailors and any other unfortunate adventurer who ventured here."

"I knew there was something evil lying within the citadel, but I had no idea it was such a loathsome beast as this," replied Splinter.

"I fear it is too late for the sailors," said Captain Jack, looking up at the twisted and charred bodies in the cocoons, left to rot awaiting the spider's attention, "but there will no more such victims now."

"As much as this was a trap," Cordelia said thoughtfully, "I still think the spider was guarding something; something at the back of the cave perhaps? Anyone coming to have a look?"

We looked at each other in trepidation of what we might find at the back of the cave, but agreed all the same that there was no point in coming all this way and turning back now.

We crept past the spider, half expecting it to come back to life at any minute, but thankfully the glow had gone out of its eyes. Bones and rotten corpses littered the back of the cave, but we pressed on holding our hands to our noses against the stench.

"Here, "said splinter, "there is a gap in the back of the cave, a passage I believe."

"Let's go have a look then."

I led the way holding the midnight skull before me.

We passed through a slimy passage that twisted and turned for a few hundred yards and eventually emerged in a vast cavern, with smooth walls and stars painted on the ceiling. In the centre of the cavern was a crystal plinth with two oval sockets.

"Are you thinking what I am thinking?" I asked the others, "That plinth must be there to hold the crystal skulls."

The rest of the party replied affirmatively.

"Then, let's place the skulls on the plinth," I continued.

With everyone agreed, I took the midnight crystal skull and placed it in the left hand socket of the plinth. It fitted perfectly.

I then placed the other smoky crystal skull in the right hand socket and everything went black.

Chapter 23 – The Twin Skulls

The blackness engulfed us with its all-consuming jet black cloak. Then from the centre of the room, there was a flicker of white light. This light expanded in a swirling cloud mixed with midnight blue. The light came from the eye sockets of the skulls, white from the smoky skull, blue from the midnight skull, merging in a central vortex spinning up from the floor of the cavern. When the vortex of light hit the ceiling the painted stars started spinning around in complex geometric patterns. Then, with a tremendous crack, the ceiling fractured down the middle letting the light escape into space. The fracture opened wider and wider until, with a tremendous boom, the cave blasted apart, sending rocks hurling outwards. Thankfully, as the blast went outwards, we were safe within the middle of the cave. Light and darkness mixed in the sky above until the light expanded so much it filled the dark void that had previously been there. Stars began to flicker into appearance and finally a moon rose over the horizon. Night had returned to the dark side and although it was still dark, we could see by the light of the moon and stars.

I remembered what the Oracle had said: "The twilight moon must be made three, for three is the order of the realm." And I wondered if this was one of the three moons that made up the twilight moon. If so I was on my way to restoring the balance of the Twilight Realm and the possibility of returning home was starting to become a reality. Those words were still very cryptic to me, however, and I still didn't understand how one moon could be made into three, but I couldn't help thinking this moon in the midnight sky could be made one of the three somehow. There was also the moon in the City of Shells and the twilight moon itself. We had three moons, but at the moment they were in three separate worlds. The answer must lie in making these worlds one, but how? The skulls held the key but there were only two skulls, so perhaps there was a third skull to be found and then the three worlds could be made one, and the twilight moon made three?

"Does anybody know if a third crystal skull exists?" I asked.

"There is something in the Codex Historicus that mentioned the possible existence of a third skull," replied Cordelia. "It says it exists in another dimension, in a parallel universe. Where that is, or what it is, I don't know I am afraid."

"I say we ask the skulls," suggested Splinter.

"You mean the skulls can speak?" I asked in wonderment.

"I can speak can't I," said Splinter indignantly, "and I am made of crystal. There is no reason why such powerful entities as the crystal skulls can't speak. I think it is more a question of whether they choose to speak."

"Well, I'll ask them then," I replied, although I was unsure quite how one addresses a pair of crystal skulls.

"Err ... Excuse me oh great skulls of power, could you impart some of your crystal wisdom and tell me where I can find the third crystal skull?"

That should do it, I thought.

The crystal skulls flickered with light through their craniums and their eyes started to glow blue and white. Then a booming voice filled the air.

"What mortal stands before us seeking that which should not be sought?"

"My name is Joshua and I seek the skull only so that the Twilight Realm may be made whole again and the twilight moon be made three."

"I see you have been talking to the master of riddles, the Oracle. That said, you have come a long way in decoding this riddle and for that you need the third skull. However it cannot be sought, it must find you."

"Then how is it to find us?" I asked.

"You must become lost before you can be found," boomed the voice.

"How are we to become lost?" I asked puzzled. But the skulls no longer spoke and the lights within them dimmed.

"We must journey back to Oceana and there try and decode this latest puzzle," said Captain Jack.

"I agree," said Splinter, "let us take these skulls and start our voyage back."

"What do you think Cordelia?" I asked.

"Yes, we must journey back. Only by travelling can we become lost, although I am not sure I understand the riddle," answered Cordelia.

"Ok, let us return to Stormchaser and set sail for Oceana," I stated. With that I led us out of the spider's lair and back to the ship.

Chapter 24 – Voyage into the Unknown

Although the ship's crew was light, we had a good captain in Captain Jack and with his instruction we managed to get Stormchaser sailing. It was hard work and I soon began to recognise the strength, the courage and the skills that sailors have. My hands blistered from pulling on the ropes and my body ached everywhere, but having recovered two skulls I felt my journey was nearing an end and if I could just keep going Trinity and I would soon return home. All we had to do was become lost; surely that was simple? I can get lost in my home town quite easily, so getting lost in a different world shouldn't take long; but I was still unsure about how the skull was going to find us.

"Do you know the way to Oceana," I asked Captain Jack.

"Yes, it is quite easy, I am using the stars to guide us."

"So, we are not lost yet?"

"Not so long as the stars shine."

"Then, let there be cloud," I said, looking up at the crystal clear sky with the stars shining so brightly you could almost touch them.

"I think you may have a long wait before there is any cloud," answered Captain Jack.

Even though we had to be lost to be found, I couldn't help thinking that we had misunderstood what was meant by becoming lost, but for the time being I concentrated my thoughts on getting lost in these strange worlds. In a way I was lost, for I could not find my way back to my own world. If that was the case, then why hadn't the other crystal skull found me so far? I could see that getting lost was going to be a whole lot more than simply losing my way.

The ship sped along under its map of stars, wind filling its sails. It was curious to me that we had a following wind both on the way and on the way back from the Citadel of Gold; it was almost as if we were being led a certain way. In that case I would keep following the path that was laid out before me, the path of least resistance, until the journey led me to where I needed to be – lost, but in what way?

I started thinking about home and how I missed my wife. I wondered what she would be doing now. Panicking, probably, as I had been gone for god knows how long, and Trinity too. I closed my eyes and held them tightly shut for a number of seconds, hoping that when I opened them I would be back home and this had all been in my imagination. Yet, when I opened them, I was still onboard Stormchaser and the stars still looked the same above me. I still struggled to get to grips with reality; was this real or all one huge psychotic experience?

"How far to Oceana?" I asked Captain Jack.

"There's no telling until we see light on the horizon; time and space don't seem to have the same meaning here."

With the moon and the stars above it wasn't quite the same as the void in which we had journeyed outwards, but still with no visible points on the horizon it almost felt as if we weren't moving. The wind through my hair and the water rushing by the ship told me otherwise, but it was still disconcerting the fact that we appeared not to be moving.

I took to standing at the prow, looking out to see if I could see any change in the horizon. It wasn't long until I was rewarded. A line of deep blue appeared on the horizon, getting brighter and brighter as we sailed on. Soon the sky ahead became the same twilight blue with which I had become so familiar since arriving in this strange realm. We crossed back into the Twilight Realm, leaving the stars behind us, sailing towards the blue moon. The journey back seemed much quicker than on the way, a phenomenon that always puzzled me; why the journey back always appeared quicker than the journey there?

The blue moon cast long shadows across the deck of the ship, which reminded me to be on the lookout for the Shadow Dancer whose sinister form was never far away when shadows were prevalent. How can one hide from such a creature, whose form was shadows themselves? I hadn't realised quite how many shadows existed until I had to try and avoid them; a near impossible task. Without shadows the world becomes two dimensional; it is shadows that give objects form and makes them three dimensional. What a strange thing shadows are, things of no substance, but without them, objects have no substance themselves.

I felt the weight of the crystal skulls in my backpack, assuring myself that they were still there. I was not going to let the Shadow Dancer get hold of them; they were things of power, power that would be used for evil purposes if the Shadow Dancer were to possess them.

I found it curious that the Shadow Dancer was so intent on capturing the crystal skulls, for the skulls being crystal barely cast any shadows themselves. I realised this was true of Splinter too and perhaps he could avoid the clutches of the Shadow Dancer. Maybe Splinter should be the bearer of the skulls, for safe keeping, until we learned how to defeat the Shadow Dancer?

As if reading my thoughts, Splinter came up alongside me and I decided upon action.

"Splinter, I have a favour to ask of you. As you have a crystal body and cast very little shadow, I think you would make an ideal guardian for the crystal skulls while the Shadow Dancer is looking for them. Would you be happy to carry them for me while we locate the third skull?"

"Why yes, of course, I have a crystal net I can carry them in if you pass them to me."

I gently removed the crystal skulls from my backpack and gingerly passed them to Splinter for safe keeping. He carefully placed them in the crystal net, which he slung over his shoulder and I was pleased to notice that his whole form, including the crystal skulls, cast very little shadow by the moonlight. This I hoped would keep the crystal skulls safe from the Shadow Dancer for the time being.

It wouldn't keep the rest of the party safe, though, and I was weary of all the many different shadows cast all around by the moonlight. How long until the Shadow Dancer strikes again, I wondered?

It wasn't long until the white and blue buildings of the port of Oceana appeared on the horizon. Standing at the prow I alerted the rest of the crew to it.

"Oceana ahead," I called.

"Full speed ahead, unfurl all sails," replied Captain Jack, "Oceana, here we come."

Stormchaser cut through the waves like a shark, skimming through the ocean with the greatest of ease; it was a master of the seas and for now the ocean was subservient to the proud vessel riding the waves.

We soon neared the harbour's entrance. Two lighthouses stood on either side of the harbour's mouth, standing like sentinels looking out to the ocean. We trimmed the sails as we entered the harbour, slowing our speed as we glided through the water. The calm water inside the harbour walls was busy with ships and boats of all shapes and sizes. There were many fishing vessels adorned with the catch of the day, nets stacked up high. I wondered what kind of vessel would be our next mode of transport. As if in response to my thoughts I heard the roar of engines from above and looked up to see a giant airship glide over the harbour towards a tall tower which I assumed was its mooring place.

"Airship above," I called in wonder.

"I've heard tell of airships," replied Captain Jack, "but never seen one yet. I would sure like to fly one," he continued with a twinkle in his eye.

"Me too," I agreed. "I vouch we take a trip over to the mooring tower when we've docked and check it out."

"Definitely, matey," replied Captain Jack, "are we all agreed?"

"Aye, aye captain," everybody responded in unison.

We soon glided into the dock with all sails down and moored next to another ship, which looked ungainly in comparison to the sleek lines of the Stormchaser. We were met by a crowd of people waiting to hear news of our voyage. Red Beard, whom I had all but forgotten about on the voyage back, soon took centre stage. For the price of a rum he was soon spinning yarns, telling tales of our voyage to the Citadel of Gold and the fearsome monsters we had encountered.

Leaving Red Beard to his grog we quietly slipped out from the crowds and made our way to the huge mooring tower standing tall on top of the hill, now with a giant airship roped to it.

Chapter 25 – The Flight of the Skylark

As we approached the tower we realised just how massive the airship was. It was at least the size of a football pitch. The balloon formed a large cigar shape with a massive rudder attached to the back and a beautiful polished wood gondola strung underneath it.

I gasped in awe of it. "It sure is big," I said.

"It is a mighty fine airship," agreed Captain Jack.

"It is beautiful," added Cordelia.

"I wonder who owns such a leviathan of the skies." I queried.

"I like that description," came a voice from behind me, "leviathan of the skies. I haven't heard that one before."

I turned to see a tall man in khaki trousers, a sheepskin flying jacket and bearing an enormous curled moustache on his face.

"In answer to your question, I am the owner of this vessel, which by the way is called Skylark."

"The Skylark sure is a beaut!" exclaimed Captain Jack. "Are you the captain as well as owner?"

"Why yes I am, Harry's the name. It's very different to sailing a ship though. I used to be a sailor."

"We've just sailed in on Stormchaser," announced Captain Jack, "after quite some adventure." At which stage Captain Jack related our story of travelling to the dark side, the Citadel of Gold and the crystal skulls.

"By Jove, that is some adventure, bravo old chaps! Can I see the crystal skulls?"

"Why yes," I replied, signalling to Splinter who came over and carefully lifted the skulls out of the crystal net bag.

"Gosh! I never thought I would see a real crystal skull; can I touch one please?"

I nodded in acquiescence.

Harry reached out and gingerly touched the fractured skull; it buzzed in recognition, flashes of light fizzing through its smoky interior.

"Goodness, I can feel real power within it. I had no idea there were two skulls."

"Yes, but there is a third and that's where we would like your help. You see we need a third skull to restore parity to the universe and heal the twilight world," I explained.

"Of course I'll help, but how?"

"Well, how well do you know the skies?"

"Like the back of my hand old chap."

"Is there any part that you haven't explored?"

"Well no ... unless of course you believe in the sky city, but that's just a myth."

"I'm beginning to believe in a lot of myths," I replied.

"Well I suppose I can take you to try and find it, but don't blame me if I get us lost."

"Perfect!" I responded. "When can we get started?"

"Well, now I suppose, it looks like you are in a hurry?"

"It's just that I have been away for quite some time and I need the skull to be able to find my way back home. My wife and family will be frantic by now."

"Well in that case, we can't leave it any longer. Follow me."

With that, Harry turned and started walking up a steel staircase built into the tower. Nodding to the others that it was okay, I turned and followed.

The spiral staircase wound round for what seemed like an eternity; the ground below became smaller and smaller. By the time we reached the top we were all out of breath, including our aeronautical leader Harry.

"Phew, no matter how many times I do it, it never gets any easier that climb," gasped Harry, trying to catch his breath.

"It sure is a tough climb," I agreed panting.

"Right-ho, all aboard who's coming aboard," said Harry as he marched across a makeshift metal bridge between the tower and the airship.

We all followed Harry to a round wooden door in the gondola. Harry inserted a large brass key and turned it. I could hear heavy bolts within the door click back in the lock, then the hiss of steam as the door automatically swung open.

"What-ho, follow me chaps." Harry stepped inside the gondola.

I followed him through into an interior like something I had never seen before. Great beams of wood arched across the curved roof and floor, like the ribcage inside a whale. Plush red leather seats lined the walls with brass portholes to look out of. At the front was a giant porthole with a ship's wheel in front of it and lots of brass levers and dials next to it. At the back was a giant steam engine with a glowing furnace being manned by an engineer. Throughout the ship a network of brass pipes filled the cabin.

"Wow, this looks like something from a Jules Verne novel!" I exclaimed.

"Jules who?" came the puzzled reply.

"Don't worry," I responded, "he was an author in my world."

Which made me wonder: Did Jules Verne ever travel to the Twilight Realm? Maybe that's where he got his inspiration from? That's if I wasn't hallucinating all of this, of course? I still wasn't sure what reality was; could my bipolar mental health condition have this much effect, conjuring up whole new worlds?

"Billy," Harry said to the engineer, "do we have full pressure?"

"Aye, sir, we have one hundred percent pressure.

"Then it's time to go; make sure the ropes are loose from the moorings Billy."

Billy went to the hatch and signalled to a man waiting at the top of the tower to release the ropes. This was duly done and Billy informed Harry, "Good to go Sir."

Harry, now at the controls and airship's wheel, pulled one lever back and then gently eased another lever forward. There was a roar from the steam engine and the sound of a propeller turning. Slowly the airship moved forwards away from the tower.

"Tally-ho, away we go," shouted Harry, above the roar of the engine. "Destination Sky City, wherever that may be? Ladies and Gentlemen, please take a seat and enjoy the journey, current altitude 100ft and climbing."

"How far are we going to climb?" I asked.

"Higher than anyone's ever been before," replied Harry. "If we are going to find Sky City, then we will have to test Skylark's aeronautical limits."

I looked down to see the blue and white buildings of Oceana, becoming smaller and smaller, rapidly receding into the distance.

"1000 feet and climbing," Harry informed us.

Soon cloud enveloped us and blocked our view.

"2000 feet and climbing," Harry kept up the commentary.

We were soon above the cloud floating on what appeared like a sea of white marshmallow below us.

"3000 feet and climbing."

The roar of the steam engine was becoming strained as we listened to the propeller struggling with the steep ascent. Billy was shovelling coal into the furnace for all he was worth.

"4000 feet and climbing."

The marshmallow clouds were now becoming distant and still we climbed.

"5000 feet and climbing."

"How high have you been before?" I hesitantly asked Harry.

"3000 feet old chap," came the reply, "never been sure if the structure would hold up if we flew any higher."

As if to emphasize his words a large groan sounded throughout the cabin as the wood beams continued to take the strain.

"Are you sure climbing this high is a good idea?" I asked.

"The Skylark will take it I hope. She's been through some rough storms in the past and held together; there must be another few thousand feet in her yet. 7000 feet and climbing."

Creaks and groans now echoed constantly throughout the airship, yet still she climbed.

"8000 feet and climbing."

"Exactly how high do you think we need to go to find Sky City?" I nervously asked.

"Not sure old chap, perhaps 30,000 feet."

"Great," I muttered.

"10,000 feet and climbing. Time to fit oxygen masks; you must all wear these at this altitude and higher."

With that Harry pulled a lever and oxygen masks dropped down above our seats. I strapped mine on and found I could speak through a microphone fitted inside.

"Will we have to wear these for the rest of the journey?" I asked.

My voice came out as if it were on a shortwave radio.

"Yes, I am afraid you do, unless you want to die from oxygen deprivation at higher altitudes that is?"

"I'll wear mine," I quickly assured him.

The sounds of wood straining became louder and louder, but still we continued to climb.

"15,000 feet and climbing. Ladies and gentlemen, we are now half way on our ascent," Harry announced with a glint in his eye.

I looked nervously at the others, who looked just as unsure as me. "Are you sure we should be pushing Skylark this high?" I asked.

"She's made of the strongest oak in the Twilight Realm; this will be a real test for her," replied Harry. "Trust me, I'll stop our ascent if I think she's going to break up. 18,000 feet and climbing."

The creaks and groans continued but didn't seem to be getting any louder, so I put my trust in Harry. I hate anything beyond my control; I'm not a control freak, but I was now in the hands of fate.

"20,000 feet and climbing."

I looked over to where Billy was frantically shovelling coal into the furnace and wondered if the steam engine had enough power to take us to 30,000 feet? It hissed and puffed, but showed no signs of slowing and the propeller kept turning.

"23,000 feet and climbing."

The heat from the engine was making the whole cabin hot, but at this height I daren't open a portal. Sweating, I wiped my brow and looked to the front of the cabin where Harry was continually pulling on levers trying to get every last bit of power from Skylark.

"25,000 feet and climbing."

I tensed with every noise the timbers made, but Skylark held sound.

"28,000 feet and climbing. Nearly there chaps, not much further to climb."

We looked at each other; all of our expressions reflected the nerves that were running through us. I looked down at my hands and noticed I had inadvertently crossed my fingers. Let's hope our luck holds out.

"30,000 feet and we have arrived at our destination altitude; I told you Skylark could do it. Bravo Skylark old bird."

"Well done Harry," I said, "now all we have to do is find Sky City."

"Not sure where that is old chap, but it has to be somewhere up here. Darned if I know where though?"

"How about we follow the moon?" suggested Cordelia. "If we keep the moon in our sight we must come across Sky City sooner or later."

"We must be nearly as high as the moon now," said Captain Jack. "Perhaps Sky City is on the moon?"

Knowing how far the moon was from the earth, I knew we could be nowhere near high enough to reach the moon.

"I don't think we are high enough for the moon, but I think Cordelia's suggestion that we head in the direction of the moon is a good one. Are we all agreed?"

"Agreed," came the communal response.

"Right-ho, setting course for the moon, Sky City here we come," said Harry

Chapter 26 – Flight at 30,000 feet

We flew through the twilight sky, which was eerily silent and had taken on a darker purplish blue hue. There were no signs of Sky City for a long time, but still we sailed on.

"Are you sure we will find Sky City up here?" I asked Harry.

"It's only a legend, but who knows?" he responded.

"I've seen many myths and legends come true already," I replied.

We floated through the purple sky; the stars and the moon seemed much brighter at this height. The tranquillity of the scene was serene and my thoughts began to drift off. My mind flew along a pathway of spiralling stars and moonbeams merging into flickering flames. I thought about the warmth of the fire burning in my hearth at home and the tears of worry falling from the big doe eyes of my wife, Jules, as she sat by the fire awaiting my return. She would be wondering where Trinity and I had gone and if we were even alive. I wanted to call out to her and give her a hug. I tried projecting my thoughts to her, saying "We are safe, we are safe," over and over again. I had no idea if she could hear my silent words, but I felt helpless and would try anything to comfort her. Oh to be able to hold her in my arms again and whisper sweet words, as lovers do, with Trinity on the floor beside us. I had to find a way back and to do so I must find the third crystal skull; only by finding the last skull would I be able restore order to the Twilight Realm and its moon.

I thought about the riddle the Oracle had set me early on in my journey: "The twilight moon must be made three, for three is the order of the realm."

This surely meant that the Twilight moon must be split into three so there would be three moons over the Twilight Realm. But why? The answer lay with the skulls, two of which we had. I knew that the third skull held the key, but how were we going to find it - or more to the point – how was the skull going to find us?

There were too many questions and not enough answers. I brought my thoughts back to the present and looked out at the stars to see if I could see any signs of Sky City. No matter how hard I looked, I could see nothing but the moon and the stars. Where oh where was Sky City and, more to the point, where was the third skull? It was certainly not proving easy locating the third skull; it was as if it didn't want to be found. I had to keep reminding myself that the skull would find me, but only if I became lost. Lost in what way though?

"Harry, have you charted a flight path for us to follow?" I asked.

"Why yes Joshua," he replied.

"And are we on it?"

"Yes, we are following the moon. Flying on moonbeams if you like."

"So we are not lost then?"

"Not so long as the moon and stars are here in the sky," responded Harry.

"I could have told you that," muttered Captain Jack.

"Fine," I replied.

Why is it, when you actually want to become lost, it's so damn hard! Even as I thought this I knew that I was looking in the wrong direction, so to speak. Deep down, I understood that becoming lost was more than just being lost on a map. The directions on a compass had little to do with the direction I had to take to become lost in the sense that the third crystal skull would find me; yet still I couldn't grasp what other way I could become lost. The crystal skull remained just out of reach; I could feel its presence, but there was something I didn't yet understand stopping it from finding me.

Cordelia did find me, however, deep in thought, "Penny for your thoughts?"

"Sorry Cordelia, I was miles away. I was just pondering how to become lost so that the third crystal skull can find us."

"I think when the time is right the skull will find us."

"But I am far from home and I need the skull to return home."

"I know, you must miss your family. I don't think, however, that we can force the issue. When the time is right we will understand what becoming lost really means."

"Time is what I have very little of. The eternal twilight of this world is deceptive, but it must be days since I set out for a walk with Trinity."

"Time may not be all that it seems in this world," said Cordelia cryptically.

"What do you mean?" I queried.

"Just that time doesn't always pass the same in this world."

I still didn't understand what Cordelia was trying to explain and my anxieties about getting home remained.

As if to echo my concerns, Trinity came up to me and gave me an unsettled glance; we both missed Jules and home.

The journey through the stars continued interminably. The stars moved in relation to the airship, but only gradually. The moon hung like a silver spotlight ahead of us, never moving or getting any nearer. We floated on the moonbeams but still there was no sign of Sky City. Anxiety built up inside me and I just wanted to scream. But what good would that do?

Cordelia in the meantime was becoming anxious about the Shadow Dancer; she had, after all, barely escaped his clutches in Old Smoky.

"I'm sure the Shadow Dancer is here with us. The shadows keep moving in strange ways," Cordelia expressed her concerns.

"I don't think he could have followed us up here, not at 30,000 feet. Even the Shadow Dancer must have his limitations," I assured her.

"I don't care what you think. It was me who he grasped earlier and I can sense him here now. Urgh, he gives me the creeps!"

"I'll watch your back for you," I said, putting a hand on her arm to assure her.

"Hmm, thanks and I'll watch yours. Mark my words though, he is here."

I looked nervously round; the deep shadows near the furnace seemed to move, but I put that down to an overactive imagination. Or was it? There appeared to be shadows within shadows; everywhere I looked the shadows flickered in unexpected ways.

Cordelia and I weren't the only ones to notice the strange activity of the shadows. Captain Jack shouted, "Look to the shadows; I believe the Shadow Dancer is here with us."

"Splinter, I called. Get into the light quickly and guard the crystal skulls from the Shadow Dancer."

Trinity, ever alert to danger, started barking at the dark shadows looming in the bowels of the airship beneath the boiler. Looking to where Trinity was directing her barks, I saw shadows stretch like inky fingers from underneath the furnace and morph into a giant jet black shadow demon with horns, forked tail and flickering tongue. In an instant the Shadow Dancer engulfed Billy, choking him and muffling his screams as he died in its hideous grasp.

Quickly we retreated to the front of the airship where we found Harry pulling levers and turning the steering wheel with frantic movements. The airship, I noticed, was starting to shake and as I looked out of the window stars came spiralling past us as we were sucked into a vortex. The ship must surely break up under this pressure; that's if the Shadow Dancer didn't get us first.

Suddenly all was silent. The silence was so complete that it was almost deafening, in a strange sort of way. With the silence came light, not from outside but from within. Every one of us glowed with an inner light, a radiant white light, so that shadows dispersed around us and never touched us. In that moment I knew what it must feel like to be an angel and wondered if I had perhaps died and gone to heaven. The light fizzed inside me and filled me with joy. Such bliss I have never known before or since.

Looking out through the front window I could see rose coloured buildings rising from the clouds. There were turrets and towers, buildings of glass and steel and slender bridges spanning the gaps between the clouds. It did indeed look like heaven and immediately I knew it was Sky City. We had found our destination and it appeared for now that we were safe from the clutches of the Shadow Dancer. Alas, the same could not be said of poor Billy, the only trace of him remaining being his flat cap and pipe on the floor near the furnace.

Chapter 27 – Sky City

Harry locked the airship's wheel in place and made his way to the back of the gondola where Billy's pipe and cap lay. The normally jovial face of Harry took on a more sombre look. He picked the pipe and cap up off the floor, his face ashen with shock.

With an air of gravity, Harry said a few words in commemoration of Billy. "Billy was a good fellow, ever loyal and hardworking. He never complained once and was always on hand when you needed him. I shall miss him dearly; the world is a much lesser place without him. May I offer his cap and pipe to the flames so that his spirit rises with the smoke and lingers in this fair place in which we now find ourselves?"

With a tear just forming in his eye, Harry tossed the pipe and cap into the furnace. "Bon voyage Billy," he said.

"Bon voyage Billy," we all echoed.

"In his memory this airship will now be known as Billy's Flier," continued Harry. With that he turned, marking the end of the makeshift ceremony.

I looked at the flames flickering in the furnace and swore to myself that somehow I would rid this world of the Shadow Dancer before I returned home.

Looking back out at the rose tinted clouds and city that lay upon them, I said, "Onwards to Sky City, we need to find the skull that cannot be found more than ever now."

Taking Billy's place, I started shovelling coal into the furnace while Harry kept us on course for the largest cluster of towers and minarets at the heart of Sky City.

From out of the clouds in front of us a golden chariot drawn by fifty swans flew in a graceful arc towards us. As it got nearer I could make out the graceful figure of the charioteer; a queen with a golden crown and robes of white. Her skin was so pale that it was almost translucent. Her face was noble and strong with fine cheekbones, as if chiselled from marble. This city of beauty was obviously inhabited by beautiful people. Like us, the queen glowed from the inside; radiant white light illuminating all around and yet keeping shadows at bay.

As she drew up alongside us she signalled us to follow her. We flew a path through towers so tall that they pierced the twilight sky and minarets so slender that you could wrap your fingers around them. Bridges arced over us as we flew under their slender spans. Clouds engulfed us in pink light as we flew through them. Our journey was one of marvels and wonders but was nothing compared to the destination itself.

A giant cloud like pink marble hung in the sky, on top of which was a glass palace shimmering with light. Sapphire turrets festooned the outside and a giant emerald dome covered the main building within the palace's outer walls. Cascading gardens sprawled from the palace abundant with cherry trees, whose pink blossom lay scattered like rose coloured jewels across the manicured lawns. Rivers of crystal clear water meandered through the gardens, running in rivulets down to the pink marble cliffs and falling as waterfalls into the sky below.

"It's beautiful," gasped Cordelia.

"It certainly is," I agreed.

We flew between the crystal turrets and towers on the outer walls to a vast marble courtyard with a huge central tower in the middle of it. The swan chariot landed gracefully on the marble courtyard while Harry dextrously manoeuvred Billy's Flier to a platform near the top of the tower. When he got within a few feet he called to me, "Joshua, take the mooring rope, open the stern door and throw the rope to the men waiting on the platform."

Doing as instructed I took the heavy rope made from coarse hemp fibre and carefully opened the stern portal. As I opened the door there was a sound like a gasp as the air rushed in. I think of it now as Billy's last gasp and hope that he found his resting place in this heavenly realm. I unfastened my oxygen mask and was relieved to find the air was pure and clear, filling my lungs with vital energy. I stepped through the door onto a roped platform on the outside of the gondola and threw the rope across to two men waiting on the tower's own platform. Soon we had safely anchored Billy's Flier and we made to depart.

The men on the tower's platform hauled us in and I was first to step off. The men bowed to me as I disembarked and with silken voices said, "Welcome to Sky City; you are the first visitors we have had here for many eons."

Trying to think of something appropriate to say, I replied in as refined a voice as I could muster:

"Greetings from the Twilight Realm. We have travelled far to be here and hope you can help us in our quest to restore unity to the Twilight Realm."

"Of your quest, I am sure there are many questions to be answered. Come, we must make our way down the tower; the queen is eager to meet you."

The greeting party spoke in unison. Turning, they entered the tower through a gothic arched doorway. Quickly we followed and found ourselves on a glass staircase spiralling down.

The glass steps played tricks with our eyes, refracting and reflecting so that they seemed to tumble into infinity. Aware of the effect this was having on us, our hosts took the first few steps slowly allowing us to acclimatise to the disorientating feeling we were experiencing. After about a dozen steps we eventually found our rhythm, finding it easier to concentrate on just one step at a time. The entire descent took about fifteen minutes, making me realize just how huge the tower must be. When we finally exited the tower we stepped onto a carpet made of cherry blossom that led to the palace at the far end of the courtyard.

As we neared the palace we could make out its spectacular features. It had a façade made up of a thousand angels carved out of glass, their wings spread as if to lift the palace into the heavens above. The glass of the palace reflected in the white marble courtyard, giving the illusion of it floating. A massive arched gateway formed the centre of the palace with filigree glass gates barring the way. Above the walls stood the huge emerald dome, bursts of dazzling green light radiating from out of it. Such beauty in a structure I have never seen before or since. I gasped and stood in awe of its splendour.

Our escort urged us on. He was adorned in emerald green robes the same colour as the dome. Soon we arrived before the gates and heard the sound of a sweet bird singing. The bird, on tiny wings of crystal, flew before us and landed on a heart shaped perch in the centre of the gate. It was like a magical key inserting itself into a lock. The song of the bird was soon ringing through the bars of the gate like a giant harp playing heaven's own melodies. Entranced by the music we watched the gates swing open before us and slowly we made our way forward between the gates of glass.

If the exterior of the palace had taken our breath away, the interior was even more spectacular. We walked through a hall of a thousand glass columns, on each side of which there were mirrors making the columns appear as if they went into infinity. Passing from this hallway we entered the main chamber of the palace. It was circular with a vast pool of water in the middle. Circumnavigating this water was a walkway with seats carved into the walls and at the far end was a throne, upon which the queen was seated. To top all this, literally, was the giant emerald dome, suspended as if on air. Emerald beams of light radiated down from it making the whole chamber glow green, including the water.

Our escort led us around the chamber to the foot of the throne where the queen rose to greet us.

"Welcome friends from afar, it has long been spoken that this day would come. You must be tired after your journey, please sit," she said, beckoning to seats either side of the throne.

With that the queen sat down. Nervously I followed suit, as eventually did all the others. Trinity, who was unaware of the formality of the occasion, curled up at the foot of the queen and began snoring loudly.

"It is a beautiful palace you have here," said Splinter, whose crystal body blended in with the glass structure.

"We are lucky that we live in such a beautiful kingdom," replied the queen. "I am being rude, as I have not yet introduced myself. I am Esmeralda, queen of Sky City."

We each introduced ourselves in turn.

After the introductions were complete, Esmeralda asked, "What brings you to Sky City?"

"We have come in search of the skull that cannot be found," I replied.

"Interesting, you speak in riddles and yet I think the answer lies not within the riddle but within yourself."

"The skull must find us, but to do that we must first become lost," I explained.

"I think that to become lost is not a physical thing. I fear you must be lost inside your mind before the skull will find you," said Esmeralda solemnly.

I knew a lot about becoming lost internally. My bipolar meant I often could not tell fact from fiction. The key must lie in my bipolar, but to get there I feared total madness. I still didn't know if I was constructing this reality around me. Perhaps I had already slipped into madness?

As if reading my thoughts, Esmeralda spoke:

"Fear not what is within; embrace it and madness cannot take hold. Fight against it and you will surely fail."

I thought back to the beginning of this journey and the red stag that had led me here and all the adventures I had had since stepping foot in the Twilight Realm. Was I walking in a dream? Should I fight my way out of it and try and wake up? The queen's words said something different; that I should embrace this reality, whatever it was.

"I can help you face your madness," said Esmeralda. "Step into the emerald pool, the Pool of Dreams. Only there will you find the answers you seek," she continued, beckoning me to enter the giant emerald pool in the centre of the chamber.

Chapter 28 – The Pool of Dreams

I looked at the glowing emerald pool and then back at the queen. She smiled reassuringly. I looked too at Trinity, who was still asleep at the Queens feet snoring loudly. I decided that I had to enter, for Trinity's sake and my wife's. We had to get back home and the only way of getting back home was to face my madness.

Getting up I took a tentative step towards the pool. I stopped, hesitating, and then asked rather embarrassedly, "Err, do I need to take my clothes off?"

The queen chuckled and said, "No, they will be dry when you come out again."

Quickly, before I changed my mind, I stepped into the water and sank like a stone.

The water engulfed me and rushed down my throat, but rather than drowning I felt my body change. Scales formed on my skin where my clothes had been. My arms and legs fused into my body and fins appeared where my hands and feet were. Gills bulged out from my neck and I started breathing the oxygen content in the water. This was the strangest feeling imaginable; I had become a fish and knew what it felt like to be a fish in water.

I experimented with my fins and soon had my tail fin moving from side to side to propel me forward. The fins on my sides helped me go up and down and from side to side. Then, like a salmon, I felt the need to swim upstream back to my birth place. I swam through memories: my marriage, my first job, my first date and down into my childhood. I remembered my schooldays and how I didn't fit in with everyone, making my own way through my adolescent years. I remembered junior school and art and paint everywhere. I always loved art and all things creative. I swam further back in time to pre-school groups and walking with a friend on a beach who lived in the same street as me. Still I swam backwards in time. I remembered crawling and my mother's face, plastic toy bricks and the cot in which I slept. Then I remembered darkness and the warmth of the wound until I was just a heartbeat and then nothing.

Thoughts started whizzing through my mind:

"Who am I?"
"What am I?"
"Where am I?"

I was confused. It was like trying to grasp the fragments of a dream; my life and consciousness had disappeared. I was lost inside myself, wherever or whatever that may be?

I remembered a fish and swimming. Was I a fish perhaps? Surely not! It didn't feel right. Yet I couldn't grasp my identity; it was as slippery as the fish I was remembering.

Then I was falling, but instead of downwards I was falling upwards. It was the strangest feeling, as though gravity was in reverse and Newton's apple was falling up towards the clouds. I tried to stop my fall but just kept moving upwards faster and faster. I screamed, but nobody could hear me. Then I stopped as suddenly as I had started. I was hovering in the air face to face with a bird on a branch. The bird was bright yellow with a round face and a hooked orange beak.

"Hello, Mr Bird," I said, "Can you tell me who I am please?"

"You're a fish … a pretty big fish I must say, which is a pity as you are too big to eat."

"Hmmm, I must say I feel like a fish, but something tells me I'm not."

"You're a fish alright; big eyes, big fins and slimy scales," said the bird.

"So, what am I doing up here?" I retorted.

"Just the question I was going to ask you," said the bird, "perhaps you fell out of the water."

"How can I fall upwards though?"

"Don't be ridiculous! Whoever heard of falling downwards?" squawked the bird.

I could see this conversation was not going to get me very far and then I fell, only this time downwards. Oh, it felt so good to be falling downwards again. Now what was it about falling at speed downwards that wasn't a good idea? Oh yes, I had it, the ground. It's not a good idea to hit the ground at speed, which I duly did. My insides splattered out into lots of little pieces. I was inside every one of those pieces, aware that I should be one but with no idea how to reassemble myself.

I heard the sound of a siren approaching, then a screech of tyres. I heard voices.

"What have we here doc?"
"Looks like a fallen salmon."
"Nasty case this, call in the assembly team."

Next thing I heard was the sound of robots hissing and clanking. Then I felt each of my individual salmon pieces being reassembled with a squelch. Soon I was whole once again, although still a salmon, which I couldn't help feeling was odd."

"Thank you," I said, with a pop from my fishy mouth.

"All in a day's work," said the doctor, "just don't go jumping from any more trees again."

"But I didn't jump; I fell upwards and spoke to a bird before falling downwards again with a splat."

"You fell upwards? Don't be ridiculous, whoever heard of falling upwards?"

As if to make a point, I suddenly fell upwards again. I'm sure I didn't used to fall this much.

Soon I was face to face with the yellow bird again.

"You again," the bird said. "Can you stop falling out of your river please, I'm trying to get some rest up here."

"But I didn't; I fell from the ground and had to be reassembled."

"Thought you looked different; no fins, or scales for that matter. In fact, what are you doing with arms and legs?"

I looked at myself and to my amazement I did indeed have arms and legs. Now this seemed more familiar; I could remember this shape, but from where?

I looked back towards the bird which had now turned into a green crystal skull and whose jaw clanked open and said, "I think you're lost, can I help you find a way back?"

"Yes please," I replied, "although I can't remember where I came from.

"That's no problem, just look into my eyes."

Nervously I gazed into the skull's green eyes and was soon enveloped in green light. I felt myself spinning down a tunnel as if I was being sucked down a plug hole and then with a splash found myself gasping for breath.

My memories came flooding back to me as I found myself back in the emerald pool inside the queen's chamber. I felt something heavy in my hand and lifted it above my head. It was the green crystal skull. Somehow I had found it, or it had found me. Carrying it carefully, I climbed out of the pool and was surprised to find my clothes dry.

"You have faced your madness in the Pool of Dreams and now the skull has found you," said Esmeralda.

"But what do I do with it now?"

"You must take it, with the other skulls, to the twilight moon," the queen replied with an air of gravity. "There you must make the twilight moon three and restore order to the realm, but the task won't be easy."

Chapter 29 – Journey to the Moon

The twilight moon had hung in the sky since I first visited the Twilight Realm; little did I know I would be visiting it, but how?

"Your majesty," I thought it best to show respect to the queen, "have you any idea of how I can get to the moon?"

"Please call me Esmeralda. I don't know exactly, but I think it may be a job for Professor Krackpov. He has his own laboratory and may be able to help build you a vehicle to reach the moon. My assistants here will escort you to his laboratory."

This signalled the end of our audience with the queen and we were escorted out, back through the glass gates of the palace and through the outer courtyard. At the far end of the courtyard there were some steps that led downwards. Our escort took us down these and through a passageway underground. At the far end of the passageway we could see light coming in from the twilight sky. It wasn't long before we exited through this opening and out into the gardens beyond. The passageway had taken us under the wall and out of the palace.

The gardens were beautiful, green grass scattered with cherry blossom from the numerous cherry trees growing there. There were also streams of water meandering through the gardens with arched wooden ornamental bridges crossing them. Our escort took us across one of the bridges in the direction of some woods.

Soon we found ourselves within the woods which were mainly made up of huge gnarled oak trees. The woods felt ancient and timeless. We followed a small track which took us deeper and deeper into the woodland. The further we went the quieter the woods became. Sweet birdsong that greeted us when we entered quickly became silent. Rustlings of small animals also faded away.

Deep in the heart of the woods we came across a massive log building, resembling a Viking hall from medieval times. This was our destination and our escort rapped on the solid oak doors of the hall.

"Who is it, who is it?" came the thin, but slightly manic voice from inside the hall.

"The queen's retinue, with some visitors for you."

"Visitors, now there's something new, I never have visitors."

"Well you have now and they are from outside Sky City!"

The doors were suddenly flung open and a wild haired, white coated gentleman of considerable age stood before them, holding a bubbling test tube in one hand and a lit match in the other.

"Outsiders, why didn't you say," cackled the old man. "Come in, come on in," he gestured, extinguishing the match in the test tube, which turned from green to orange, then to yellow and finally to red as it went pop.

We all looked surprised but the old scientist just ignored us and turned and went back inside. We all followed, apart from our escort, who bid us goodbye and left to return to the queen.

Inside the great hall was lit by sodium flares with great arched beams supporting the roof. The place was awash with test tubes, machinery and all kinds of unusual scientific equipment. The place was chaotic and untidy, but in keeping with 'the mad scientist'.

He led us to a great table in the middle of the hall, which was also covered in scientific equipment, and beckoned us to sit. This we did, after removing whatever apparatus was on the chair. I removed a strange looking helmet with dials on the side and a sun visor.

"Well, what brings you to Sky City?" the professor asked.

"We came in search of the skull that can't be found," I answered, showing him the skull.

"Well you seem to have found it then."

"It found me," I replied, "when I was lost in the Pool of Dreams."

"Lucky it found you," I should say, "you could still be there lost in madness now if not!"

"I know," I said, "it was an unsettling experience."

"So now you have the emerald skull, why have you sought me out?"

"We need to take it, with the other crystal skulls, to the twilight moon and hoped you may be able to help us get there."

"Ha, ha," chuckled the professor, with a glint in his eye. "You are going to need a special vehicle to reach the moon and as it happens I have been building one these past few years. Come follow me," he beckoned.

With that the professor took us to a back door in the hall, somewhat smaller than the front doors and out into the woods again.

"Heehe, I knew it would be used sometime," cackled the professor. As to what he was referring we had no idea.

We began to climb, the woods getting thinner and thinner, until we came to a clearing. In the middle of the clearing was a huge scaffold tower with something that resembled a rocket fastened to it. I say resembled a rocket for it was not smooth and polished like the lunar module that Neil Armstrong took to the moon; on the contrary it was a patchwork of a variety of sheets of metal bolted together in a haphazard way. Yes, it was round, tall and pointed, but its structure resembled a patchwork quilt.

"Behold, Starshooter! Not even the queen knows this exists."

"Err, very nice rocket you have there," I said nervously.

"Why thank you, it took years to build. When it is fuelled all I need to do is light the engines and vaboom! Off she goes. I am so glad you will be riding in her," he said to me.

"Err, has she ever been tested?" I asked.

"Oh no, you only get one chance with this baby. Can't test her, but I know she will work!"

"Oh," I replied uncertainly, "how many people can fly in her?"

"Just two," answered the professor, "you and your dog will be fine," he said with a manic grin.

"Trinity! You can't take a dog to the moon!" I exclaimed.

At which point Trinity barked and the professor said, "Don't worry, I will soon have a space suit made for her."

I could see I wasn't going to win this argument and I must say I didn't want to be separated from Trinity. "If you insist," I said, resignedly.

There followed a period of weeks of training; getting to know the controls of the rocket and the module we would be landing on the moon with. Trinity loved her space suit and wouldn't go out walking without wearing it. She looked so cute in her little white suit and big round helmet.

Eventually launch day came and to say I was nervous was an understatement. Despite gaining an understanding of how the rocket worked and knowing all the controls, I couldn't help thinking what a rickety piece of machinery it was. Still I had no choice; I had to go to the moon in order to make the twilight moon three and to find our way home again.

While the others waited a safe distance away we climbed the launch tower and opened the hatch in the nose cone of the rocket. Trinity leapt in first and the professor belted her in to her little doggy seat. I followed and belted myself in. I shut the hatch and looked through the round portal to where the professor waited a few hundred feet away. Nervously I gave the ignition signal, a thumbs up through the window.

Not hesitating, the professor struck a match and lit a fuse that cracked and sparkled as the flame made its way to the rocket's burners. After a few seconds I heard a boom as the engines ignited and then I was flung back into my seat as the rocket lifted off.

My face went like jelly as ripples of g-force spread across it and I looked out of the cockpit to see Sky City rapidly disappearing behind me. We were on our way, next stop the moon!

The sky turned from blue, to purple, to black and the planet below took the form of a beautiful blue green marble. I suddenly felt like a god looking down on his creation. What an amazing perspective it gives you on the world, even if it was not my world. Or was it? Was the world I was looking down on really my world but with two different realities? One was the twilight world and one was earth as I knew it. I was finding it all hard to take in and wasn't sure what was real anymore.

Now that we were in outer space proper the g-force I had felt on take-off subsided.

Space, I decided, was beautiful. The stars were like bright diamonds in the sky. It felt more like sailing than being in a rocket as we drifted through the stars. Trinity, on the right hand side of me, similarly looked entranced as she looked out of her little doggy helmet through the portal at the stars and the planet below. She was a natural dogonaut.

My mind drifted towards home again. Was I really flying through space at thousands of miles an hour or was my mind playing tricks on me? I had always struggled to distinguish what was real and what was not. Reality, I decided at that point in time, is whatever you perceive it to be, not what someone else would have you believe. I contemplated whether my community psychiatric nurse, Alana, would agree with my concept of reality. Maybe I could discuss this with her on her next visit when I eventually got back home.

I was missing my wife, Jules, more than ever now. How she must be worrying. I hoped I would be back with her soon and that I was now on the final stretch of my journey.

The journey to the moon was quicker than I expected and it wasn't long until it came into view; bigger and brighter than I had ever seen it before. How strange that I should be heading for the moon in a patchwork, tin can rocket. Not only that, but a moon in a different world to the one I had left behind oh so long ago.

I turned off the main rockets; it would soon be time for the boosters as we neared the moon. Following the professor's instructions, as the moon came within range, I manoeuvred the rocket with the boosters into a geo-stationary orbit around the moon. We had arrived and it was now time to deploy the landing module.

Chapter 30 – Lunar Adventure

I looked at the variety of levers before me. It was time to separate the landing module from the command module. I turned the levers: One, two, three in the sequence the professor had taught me. There was a hiss, like a gasp, as the landing module separated from the command module, which would stay in geo-stationary orbit whilst Trinity and I were on the moon.

I fired the boosters in the landing module to take us out of orbit and then the gravity of the moon started pulling us in. Slowly we descended, the moon getting bigger and bigger below us. Our speed increased and the surface of the moon loomed towards us. I fired our booster rockets to slow us down and gently the moon came nearer and nearer. I could see the craters pockmarking the surface and steered us with the booster rockets to a flat area on which to land.

Soon the moon was within a few hundred feet of the landing module. I fired the boosters again and started counting down: ten, nine, eight, seven, six, five, four, three, two, one.

"The Beagle has landed," I announced. We had called the landing module 'The Beagle' as we had a dog on board, even though Trinity was a Staffie.

I turned the handle to open the hatch and lifting Trinity in my arms climbed down the steps. Once we were on the bottom rung, I decided a few words were appropriate as we stepped off.

"One small step for a man, one giant leap for canine kind."

With that we stepped off and Trinity bounded across the moon's surface like a dog on a pogo stick. The gravity on the moon was only one sixth of the earth's and we walked in giant strides across the surface.

Having acclimatised to the moon's gravity, I lowered the lunar buggy down from the module and sat behind the wheel with Trinity next to me.

Just as I did so I saw shadows move from under the module. Somehow, the Shadow Dancer had followed us to the moon. I looked back at the skulls on the back seat and then floored the accelerator.

The shadows stretched like inky fingers towards us, but with my foot flat to the floor they stayed just out of reach. I knew there was only one way of avoiding the clutches of the Shadow Dancer: I had to get to the dark side of the moon.

The journey was bumpy beyond belief and many a time we jumped over the edge of craters, the low gravity making this possible, but still the shadows chased us. Faster and faster we went, kicking up dust all along. Somehow, the shadows chasing us became faster still and it was only a matter of time before they would swallow us up.

I looked back and to my horror saw the shadow start to engulf the moon buggy, but just before it did we went into total blackness; we had reached the dark side of the moon.

I put my arm out and touched Trinity to make sure she was there and then lifted the skulls from the back of the moon buggy. We were free of the Shadow Dancer for now for there were no shadows, only darkness. But what was I to do with the skulls now we were here?

I took them out onto the moon and they started to glow. Momentarily panic stricken, I thought that they were going to cast shadows. They shone with such brilliance, however, that no shadows were able to get within a few hundred feet of us. Thankfully the sun visors on our helmets protected us from their full glare as they got brighter still. Then something magical happened: the moon began to shift.

I could feel the ground beneath us moving. This must be the moon splitting into three, I thought. Trinity, aware that there was danger, jumped off her seat and onto the accelerator. We had to get back to the landing module before the moon cracked apart totally. Leaving the skulls where they were we sped across the breaking up surface and back to the lunar module.

A number of times the ground opened up before us and we literally flew over chasms, landing with just inches to spare. When we eventually arrived at the module it was tilted to one side as the ground had shifted under one of the landing pods.

I grabbed Trinity and quickly climbed the steps of the lunar module. Once inside I wasted no time in firing the engines. Because of the angle we were at, we lifted off and nearly crashed straight back down again. It was only with a jerk of the control stick that I managed to straighten it just in time. Soon we were a few hundred feet up and could see the moon splitting into three before our eyes. The power of the crystal skulls was awesome.

We blasted further and further away from the surface and were soon within reach of the command module. With some tricky manoeuvring we managed to dock with the command module and were soon back inside the main cabin. Quickly I ignited the main thrusters and took us out of orbit from the splitting moon and heading towards the home planet once more.

From a safe distance we watched the moon complete its transformation into three and soon there were three moons in the sky. It felt so strange to be looking back at three moons.

We re-entered the Twilight Realm's atmosphere, flames burning up around our capsule. Keeping course for Sky City we opened the main chutes to slow our descent. When we had reached the altitude of Sky City we were amazed to find it wasn't there. The answer to the missing city came far below, at ground level. With the splitting of the moons into three Sky City had returned to ground level, its palaces and pink marble cliffs still intact.

We were greeted by our companions on landing who, having checked that we were still intact, started asking questions about the moon. I told them about our adventure, but the one question we couldn't answer was what had happened to the Shadow Dancer? I could only hope it was destroyed with the splitting of the moons, but I had an uneasy feeling it was still around.

Chapter 31 – The Return of the Shadow Dancer

"We must journey back," I said, "but I still don't know the way."

"The red deer will find you; when it does, make sure you follow it," said Splinter.

Just then I saw a shadow move unexpectedly. I turned around and saw the deepest, darkest, blackest shadow I had ever seen and it was expanding and coming towards me. I had no time to flee before it was upon me.

The shadow felt cold and slimy, filling my body like a black slime. I felt myself choking and then lost consciousness. Except that an inner spark in me kept glowing. I could feel the evil inside me; desperation and dread filled me to the core and I felt myself falling down a bottomless pit of despair. A pit I had been in a thousand times before as part of my bipolar; a pit I had fought out of before.

In that deep dark lonely place I saw the real form of the Shadow Dancer come towards me. A fiend, with horns and a forked tail.

"Welcome to my domain," it said with a hideous chuckle, "may your miserable soul rot here forever," it continued.

"It is not as miserable as your decrepit soul," I retorted.

"You pay me too many compliments," the Shadow Dancer lashed back in response.

"I've been in worse places than this," I replied, knowing what I had been through when my bipolar mood dipped to its lowest.

"You will die here, you can't escape my clutches."

With that it threw its hands forward and yet more dark shadows engulfed me.

Wave upon wave of darkness and woe hit me; how was I to survive in this miserable place? Further and further I was dragged down into the depths of despair until I couldn't go on any longer. The little life left in me slowly started to fade away.

With barely a pulse in my body I heard a distant bark. What was that? Why was it important to me? Then slowly I remembered Trinity and how much I loved her. Trinity brought back memories of Jules, which I grasped onto. The love I felt for Jules and Trinity was like a lantern in the dark. Quickly the light expanded so that it enveloped me and spread outwards.

"No, this can't be happening," I heard the Shadow Dancer gasp. "No one has ever escaped my clutches before."

Hearing the Shadow Dancer's evil voice, I focused the light on it and let love expand it into an arrow that sped into the shadow demon with force.

The Shadow Dancer screamed like a thousand dying banshees. It howled and it bellowed and still I made the light shine into it until there was a huge explosion and the Shadow Dancer shattered into a million dark pieces, never to bother anyone again.

Slowly I woke, coughing and choking, with Trinity licking my face.

"Trinity, Trinity, my ever faithful dog … you saved me from the Shadow Dancer and helped rid this world of that horrific demon.

Splinter and Cordelia helped me up, concern in their faces.

"Don't worry, I am fine, the Shadow Dancer is no more and the twilight moon is now three. It is now time for the red stag to return and lead us home. Trinity and I have been too long away and we are missing Jules so dearly."

Chapter 32 – Search for the Stag

"We must journey to the red woods; that is where the red stag is to be found. Only amongst those giant trees will we find such a mighty stag," said Splinter.

"Do you know where the red woods are?" I asked.

"They lie to the north where the great mountains lie," Splinter replied.

"May we hitch a ride on Billy's flier?" I asked Harry.

"I am afraid Billy's flier is in need of repair," Harry said apologetically. "The flight to Sky City took its toll; it will take months to overhaul."

"Are there any trains we can take to the great mountains?" I enquired.

"No, the great mountains are a wilderness; the only way there is on foot I am afraid," Splinter replied.

"Then, on foot we go. Who's coming with me?"

Everyone apart from Harry, who had to repair his airship, volunteered to go. I felt such gratitude towards them in this world so far from my own; they had become real friends who had stood by me all the way.

Before we left, Harry checked on his radio in Billy's flier for any news following the twilight moon becoming three. There was indeed; as well as Sky City returning to the Twilight Realm, the City of Shells had risen from the deep and was now an island in the ocean. It was as if there were three moons, one for each realm: the Twilight Realm; the City of Shells and Sky City. Order had indeed been restored.

We all bid farewell to Harry and thanked him for all he had done for us. Then we turned and headed northwards.

We soon left the pink cliffs and arched bridges of Sky City behind and made our way towards the wilderness in the north. The land became more rugged and hilly.

The journey through the hills seemed to go on forever; each time we topped one hill, another would come into view. How long until we see the mountains with their redwoods, I wondered?

I thought about home once again. I had succeeded in my task and made the twilight moon three yet still it seemed I had to wait until I returned home. Would this journey never end? I missed my wife and home so much. What if I couldn't find the red stag and was stuck here forever? What if this was all a conjuration of my mind and the red stag was something locked deep inside it, never to be released? Had madness engulfed me? Was all this the mechanisms of a decaying mind?

All these questions were spinning round in my head which obviously showed in my worried expression.

Splinter noticed the look of fear and uncertainty on my face and put his crystal arm around me. "We have travelled a long way together through many dangers. Don't worry, we will find the red stag and return you home in safety."

Cordelia echoed his words: "It must be hard for you being away from home for so long but we will find your red stag I promise you. You will get home, of that I have no doubt."

Captain Jack, who can be a man of few words, said "Aye, we will get you home." And patted me on the back.

The hills became rocky and damp. Moss formed on the rocks, making our footing treacherous and slippery, but we carried on regardless, determined to find the redwoods and stag.

As we clambered through these rocks and boulders, the path we were on forked with one path going north west and the other one north east. We stopped, not sure which way to go. Between the two paths stood a tree. I looked up and saw a familiar face, one that I hadn't seen for a long time. It was the leprechaun I had encountered at the start of the journey and like the last time I saw him he was laughing away.

"It's alright for you to laugh," I said to the cheeky little leprechaun above me in his curled up boots, green britches with silver buckle, red waistcoat and pointed green hat. "Can you tell me which path I should take to the red woods please?"

"Lost are you?"

"I have been lost since I started on this damnable journey," I retorted.

"Well, maybe I can help, or maybe I can't?"

"Why does everyone speak in riddles in this twilight world?"

"The truth is dangerous and riddles are but a cloak to keep it safe," came the even more cryptic reply.

I could see I wasn't getting anywhere, but pressed on regardless. "Please, just tell me which path to take?"

"If you insist," but be careful in your choice. "The left path leads to danger and is known as the path of the dead. The right path leads to beauty and light and is known as the path of the spirit."

"What is that supposed to mean," I asked, looking up at the leprechaun, but when I looked he was gone. He had vanished into thin air and was nowhere to be seen.

"Can anyone make out this riddle?" I asked. "Which way should I go?"

"I am afraid it means nothing to me," said Splinter, "but be careful of a Leprechaun's riddle, they are not always what they seem."

"Yes, be careful in your choice," echoed Cordelia.

"What do you think, Captain Jack?" I asked.

"Follow your instinct, that's all I can say," he replied.

From the riddle the right path sounded more attractive, but my instinct told me that this was a trap. Quickly, before I changed my mind, I strode out onto the left path. The others, hesitantly, followed me.

The path quickly wound upwards and we found ourselves struggling for breath. After many hours' arduous climb we found ourselves on a marshy plateau. I looked down the way we had come and could clearly see now where the path to the right went. It sloped gently up through fields of buttercups and daisies and then entered some mist that shone a radiant white. I could see, through gaps in the mist, a drop seemingly without a bottom. This was what was meant by the path of the spirits, because only spirits and eagles could fly over that chasm; had we tried we would surely have fallen to our deaths and our spirits would be joining that mysterious white mist. I had hoped with the splitting of the moon into three my twilight journey of danger would have ended. It appeared not and until I found the stag to lead me out of this world danger was ever present.

There was a thin trail leading across the marsh so, having no other options, we set off upon this trail. The marsh stank of rotting vegetation and the further into the marsh we went the stronger the smell got. The stench was so strong that it made it difficult to breathe.

As we crossed the marsh I couldn't help but feel that we were being followed and kept looking back to see if I could see anything. No matter how hard I looked, however, I couldn't see anyone following us and so kept walking onwards wearily.

Green mist began to rise up from the marsh and swirl around our feet. It was cold and clammy, like dead fingers. Cordelia shuddered and said, "This place gives me the creeps."

"Me too," I agreed, choking on the fetid air.

Dark sketchy figures appeared in the mist before us moving slowly and woodenly. I didn't like the look of them and turned to see if I could find a way around them. Whichever way I turned there were more dark figures; we were surrounded and they didn't look too friendly.

"What now?" I asked the others in desperation.

"I'm not sure," said Captain Jack, "but in this foul smelling place they can only be evil."

"Great!" I replied.

Soon the figures were near enough for us to distinguish that they were zombies, some with missing limbs, covered in swamp goo.
"Err, yak!" exclaimed Cordelia.

"That's no way to greet the citizens of the swamp now is it?" said a zombie in a rasping wet voice, who appeared to be their leader.

"Err... Hello," I said tentatively.

"That's better," rasped the lead zombie, "it's good to have some warm flesh and blood in the swamp with us," he chuckled. "Flesh and blood, yum, yum!"

"Quick," said Captain Jack, "we have to run for it. Follow me, I'll cut a way through these rotten pieces of meat."
With that Jack drew a sword and ran forward, chopping the lead zombie in half. The two halves separated but the top half kept trying to grab Jack as he ran by, while the bottom half kept walking on.

Splinter also took to the front, slashing at the zombies with his razor sided hands. Zombie pieces were flying everywhere as Cordelia and I followed. I felt a cold clammy hand grasp me; I looked and saw that it wasn't attached to a body and yanked it off me.

Soon we had broken through the zombies and were running clear; now I knew why it was called the path of the dead. We kept running for what seemed like an eternity and when we finally exited the swamp lay gasping on the rocky ground. We had made it to the great mountains.

Chapter 33 – The Redwoods

At the foot of the mountains lay a great forest. We followed a path through the rocks and into the forest. The trees were like giants; huge redwood trees that were as wide as a house and towered hundreds of feet above us, piercing the sky with their bushy tops. The scent of pine filled the air and invigorated us after the stench of the swamps. We were here at last; now all we had to do was find the red stag. Instead an old man came walking towards us.

This was no ordinary old man, though, for he had about him a cloak made of leaves and even his face seemed to sprout leaves. Upon his head he wore a crown of antlers.

"Greetings," he said, in a voice like the summer wind. "Welcome to my forest; you have come a long way."

"Thank you," I replied, "would you happen to know of a giant red stag?"

"That I do," the old man chuckled, "for the stag is I. Some people know me as Hearn the Hunter, some people as the Green Man. When I choose I gallop out as a stag and travel between worlds keeping nature in harmony. You, young man, have journeyed far since you followed me into this realm, now is the time to journey back."

With these words the Green Man morphed before my eyes and turned into a beautiful red stag. Dipping its antlers towards me it turned and ran. I quickly said goodbye to my companions and then turned and ran after the stag, with Trinity in the lead bounding on.

The redwoods seemed to blur and fade around us and then we stumbled through some oak woods that I never thought I would see again. We were back on the walk we had left all that time ago. I looked back up the path and saw the stag, high on a hill, bow its head majestically towards us and then it turned and disappeared into the forest beyond.

We returned to the car and I drove home in a trance, all the time thinking about Jules and how pleased I would be to see her again; yet concerned about how stressed she must be with our prolonged absence.

We arrived back home and I let myself and Trinity in. Nothing seemed out of the ordinary and when I called to Jules to announce our arrival home, she came running down the stairs.

"Did you have a nice walk sweetheart? Dinner is nearly ready," she said, giving me a hug. At which point Trinity leapt on Jules, nearly bowling us both over. "And you too," Jules laughed, giving Trinity a tummy rub.

I was lost at the normality of it all; how come Jules wasn't panicking and dinner was nearly ready? I glanced at the paper lying on the coffee table; it was the same paper, same date that I had left there just before I went out.

Jules looked at me, "Is something wrong love?"

"Well … no nothing."

Twi